EV
Richards
Harrison

2 7 DEC 2012

15/07/16
17/1/17
Lawrence
24/02/20

Morgan
RD

Please return on or before the latest date above.
You can renew online at *www.kent.gov.uk/libs*
or by telephone 08458 247 200

Libraries & Archives

BOHEMIAN RHAPSODY

Elfie Summers is an archaeologist with a pet hate of private collectors. Cue Gabriel Carter, a self-made millionaire. He invites Elfie to accompany him to Prague to verify the authenticity of an Anglo-Saxon buckle, said to grant true love to whoever touches it. And whilst Gabriel's sole motive is to settle an old score, Elfie just wants to return to her quiet, scholarly life — but the city and the buckle have other ideas . . .

SERENITY WOODS

BOHEMIAN RHAPSODY

Complete and Unabridged

LINFORD
Leicester

First published in Great Britain in 2011

First Linford Edition
published 2012

British Library CIP Data

Woods, Serenity.
  Bohemian rhapsody. - -
  (Linford romance library)
  1. Love stories.
  2. Large type books.
  I. Title II. Series
  823.9'2–dc23

  ISBN 978–1–4448–1039–4

Published by
F. A. Thorpe (Publishing)
Anstey, Leicestershire

Set by Words & Graphics Ltd.
Anstey, Leicestershire
Printed and bound in Great Britain by
T. J. International Ltd., Padstow, Cornwall

This book is printed on acid-free paper

1

Dr Elfleda Summers unplugged her laptop from the projector and began putting it into its case. The bell had just rung and her students were shuffling their way out of the lecture theatre. Elfie zipped up the computer bag and then looked up at the rows of seats rising before her.

He was still there.

She pushed her glasses up her nose and studied him, frowning. She had spotted him as soon as she walked into the lecture theatre that morning, sitting amongst her eighteen-year-old students, oblivious to their whispers as he studied the screen of his iPad. Who was he? He didn't look anything like a student, with his smart navy business suit, crisp white shirt and elegant tie; not even the type of person usually interested in archaeology.

1

He had watched her thoughtfully throughout her lecture, and she had to admit her gaze had strayed to him more than once. Now she observed him as he came down to the front row and leaned on the bench, smiling.

'Can I help you?' she asked coolly, unnerved by his warm brown eyes.

'Good afternoon, Dr Summers,' he replied, and formally offered her his hand. 'I am Gabriel Carter.'

It would be impolite to refuse his hand so she took it, accepting the handshake with a firm grip of her own. His skin was warm and brown against the white sleeve of his shirt. Was it her imagination, or did he hold her hand slightly longer than was necessary?

He stepped back. 'Do you have a moment to talk?'

'Yes. My next lecture is at two o'clock.'

He nodded. 'I'm here to ask you about the Buckle of Bohemia.'

She laughed, but he didn't laugh back. Her smile faded. 'You're serious?'

He leaned back and crossed his arms. 'What do you know of it?'

She shrugged. 'It's a myth, put around by Victorian treasure hunters. There's no evidence to support its existence.'

'Humour me for a moment. What can you tell me of its history?'

She was tempted to say that she studied archaeology, not fantasy, but realised that he was genuinely interested in finding out what she knew, and she sighed. 'It's supposedly a twin to the Buckle found at Sutton Hoo. It was given to one of the kings of France and passed down to Charlemagne. He fell in love with a Bohemian Princess and allegedly gave the Buckle to her as a symbol of his love, because he was already married and knew that they could never be together. The myth goes that if you find it and touch it, it will bring you true love.' She finished with a snort.

Gabriel smiled. 'You don't believe in true love?'

'I don't believe in the power of an

artefact to grant it.' She laughed at his raised eyebrow. 'You can't seriously believe that a piece of polished metal has the power to grant happiness?'

'Charlemagne was said to have been crazed with love for Princess Libuse. It wouldn't surprise me if just a little of that passion rubbed off on the Buckle,' he said.

Elfie's eyes narrowed. 'You know about the Buckle? So why ask me?'

'I wanted to see what you knew.'

'And did I pass the test?' she asked quietly.

His brown eyes were very intense. 'Oh yes,' he said, just as softly.

She looked him up and down. 'Forgive me if I sound rude, but you don't look the sort of person to be interested in dusty artefacts.'

'Archaeologists don't always come with hairy beards and stripy jumpers.'

'Are you an archaeologist?' she asked, her heart giving a strange leap.

'Well, no, actually, I work with computers. I'm a private collector.'

Disappointment washed over her. 'Oh.'

'I've upset you,' he frowned.

'I'm afraid that collectors are on a par for me with traffic wardens.'

'That bad, eh?' He smiled wryly. 'Why is that so? It's people like me that often find some of the more rare items that were considered lost forever.'

'Well I'd love to own a bit of history, a ring worn by Richard the Third, or a part of the Sutton Hoo treasure. But I believe that our past belongs to everyone, not to an individual. Artefacts should be on display in museums for everyone to see, not in private collections for the pleasure of one person.' It was something she felt very passionate about.

He nodded. 'I see. As it so happens, I am opening a museum, although only a very small one.'

She studied him. 'Will you charge people to go in?'

'Yes. The money will go to a cancer charity.'

'Oh.' Well that wasn't quite so bad, she thought, but still she had to disagree with the general way he was going about it.

Now he changed the subject by saying: 'I'm here for a meeting with your Head of Department.'

'With David? What about?'

'Actually it's about you.'

'Me?'

'Yes, Dr Summers, you. I'd like you to be there, of course. We arranged to meet at eleven thirty in his office. Would you come?'

Elfie thought quickly. She was the leading expert on Anglo-Saxon jewellery in the south of England so it was presumably about some Anglo-Saxon artefact. She wanted to turn him down. Private collectors were selfish and egocentric and she didn't want to share the same air as one of them.

But still, she was only being asked to go to a meeting, not to marry the guy. 'Okay,' she said finally.

'Good.' His brown eyes studied her, a hint of a smile in their depths. 'You're quite amazing,' he said out of the blue.

She was completely taken aback by the compliment and blinked at him for a moment. 'I presume you mean my lecture.'

He pretended to think for a moment as he studied her. She watched his eyes run briefly down her figure and come back to rest on her red hair. 'That as well,' he said, and she felt her cheeks grow uncharacteristically hot. There was definitely a smile in his eyes now.

There was a knock on the door of the lecture theatre and Elfie jumped, startled. A woman walked in, about the same age as her; twenty five, give or take. The woman looked as incongruous in the university setting as Gabriel did. She wore a very well cut, plum-coloured suit with a neat white blouse that offset her jet black, tumbling hair to perfection. Her high-heeled shoes matched her suit, and as she came nearer, Elfie could see that her make-up was heavy but immaculate, and her nails were long and polished.

Elfie felt like a tramp meeting a princess.

Gabriel said, 'This is Sasha, my PA. Sasha, this is Dr Elfleda Summers.'

'Everyone calls me Elfie,' said Elfie, as she always did, then wished she hadn't, as it sounded like a pathetic attempt to be friendly with the woman.

'It's a strange name,' Sasha observed bluntly as they formally shook hands. 'Is it German?'

'Anglo-Saxon. My father was an archaeologist too.'

Sasha nodded politely, but Elfie had the feeling she hadn't really been listening. She suddenly saw herself as the other woman must see her — an old maid, frumpily dressed, peering over the top of her glasses. She reddened again.

However the PA had turned her attention to Gabriel, a mobile phone in her hand. 'You left this in the car. It's Craig; he wants a quick word about the New York meeting next week.'

'Okay.' Gabriel gave Elfie a smile. 'I'll meet you at David's office?'

'Sure.' Elfie watched them leave and

then collected her laptop. On the way to her office, she stopped by the ladies. Standing in front of the full-length mirror inside, she studied her reflection.

What had Gabriel made of her? He was used to the immaculate Sasha, she reminded herself. She looked at her scruffy jeans, the over-large, shapeless jumper and flat shoes. Her hair was pulled off her face in a ponytail and there was not a trace of make-up on her skin. Her glasses gave her a distinctly 'bookish' appearance.

Slowly, she took the glasses off and pulled out the scrunchie that restrained her hair. It spread across her shoulders like a sheet of fire. Elfie had always hated the colour, having put up with horrible nicknames at school, like 'carrot-head'. When she was younger, though, her father had told her that it was beautiful. 'It's Titian,' he used to say. 'Ginger doesn't have gold highlights like yours. You should be proud of it, not hide it away. It's the colour of great Kings and Queens, Elfie.'

With her hair loose and no glasses, she already looked more glamorous, more feminine, just as her father had said she would. But, as usual, thinking of her father soured her mood, and quickly she pulled all her hair back into the scrunchie and replaced the glasses.

This was the way she chose to dress, she reminded herself. After all, the main reason that women wore make-up and fancy clothes was to attract a man, and attracting a man was one thing that Elfie was not interested in. If she wanted to look like a fashion model, she told herself firmly, she should have gone to work for Vivienne Westwood.

She put the thought of Gabriel's warm smile to the back of her mind, reminding herself that he was a private collector, and picked up her laptop.

Dropping the computer off in her room, she walked along the corridor to David Parsons' office. Gabriel was already there, and to Elfie's surprise so was Luke Matherson, a lecturer in

Roman studies. Luke was Australian by birth, blond, fit, athletic and good looking — and he knew it.

Luke nodded as she walked in. 'Queen Elizabeth.' The Virgin Queen — the nickname he had given her after she had turned him down when he invited her out for dinner, and it never failed to irritate her, not in the least because, although she would never admit it to anyone, his nickname was surprisingly accurate — in the not-having-had-sex-yet part, anyway.

'Revolting peasant,' she retorted to Luke. She pretended not to notice Gabriel hiding a smile behind a hand.

She took the only armchair left in the small office. On the centre of the coffee table was a Christmas decoration. It was only two weeks until December the twenty-fifth and nearly the end of term.

'Thanks for coming, Elfie,' said David. 'I understand that you've already met Gabriel Carter.'

'Yes.'

'Well Gabriel has a proposition to put

to you both. Gabriel, if you would?'

'Of course.' Gabriel smiled at her. 'I have something I would like you to examine and authenticate for me.'

'Oh?' Elfie's eyes flicked over to his briefcase, wondering what precious relic he was hiding in there.

'It's not here,' he said, amused. 'It's in Prague.'

'Prague?'

'Yes, in a private collection.'

Realisation sunk in slowly, like a stone dropped into treacle. 'You're talking about the Buckle of Bohemia again, aren't you?'

Gabriel just grinned. His eyes stayed on hers, alight with the excitement that she was just beginning to feel.

She shook her head, trying not to get her hopes up. 'But it's just a myth. It doesn't really exist.'

He leaned forward then, unable to contain his enthusiasm. 'Think about it, Elfie. Legend says Raedwald gave it to the French kings, and therefore Charlemagne would have inherited it. It's perfectly plausible that he could have met Princess Libuse, and it's also possible that they fell in love. If he did give it to her, then it makes sense to think it's still somewhere in Prague.'

'I suppose. But what makes you think you've found it?'

He sat back in his chair. 'I believe it's being held in a collection belonging to Václav Doležal. He's a private collector too, a rather more unscrupulous one than myself, I may add; he doesn't always acquire his treasures legally.'

'Does he live in Prague?'

'He bought Karlstein Castle a few years ago — it's about sixteen miles from Prague — the Czech king Charles IV lived there during the fourteenth century, and most of his private collection is there.'

'Do you know him well?' She sensed from the way his eyes had grown dark that although the man was an old acquaintance, he was not a friend.

'We go back some way, yes. We've almost come to blows on several occasions when we've both gone for the same artefact.'

'You're a regular Indiana Jones, aren't you?' she said, unable to suppress her annoyance at the thought of two men arguing over some relic that should have been in a museum in the first place.

Gabriel said nothing, but David shot her a warning glance. She sighed. 'So what makes you think this . . . Doležal fellow will give you the Buckle — if he has it, which I very much doubt — if you are old adversaries?'

Gabriel shrugged. 'I intend to offer him a substantial amount of money.'

To a guy who lived in a castle, Elfie mused, a substantial amount of money must mean a very different thing to what it meant to her. 'I still don't understand what you want me for.'

'For verification, of course. If the Buckle is there, I want you to tell me if it's the real thing.'

'So you want me to go to Prague with you?'

'Yes. This Friday, for the weekend.'

She blinked. 'Tomorrow? Can't it wait until the end of term?'

'No. I've made arrangements to have your lectures covered. You'll have full expenses, everything paid for.'

She stared at him, confused by her complex emotions. She had felt a jolt of excitement, like the snap of static electricity, at his exotic invitation. However she also felt irritated that he had just assumed that she would go with him. The thought of spending ten more minutes, let alone a weekend, with a private collector was quite abhorrent to her, even if the collector was tall and dark with gorgeous brown eyes.

He smiled at her. 'Prague is very beautiful, especially at this time of year. I'm sure you'd love it.'

Who was he to say what she would or wouldn't love? 'I don't know, I'm very busy,' she said tartly.

Luke threw his hands into the air. 'Oh, for God's sake, Elfie, what's your problem? A free trip to Prague and a chance to have a look at some ancient relics? Of course you'll go! What I want to know is, what am I doing here?'

Gabriel cleared his throat. 'Of course I would not expect Dr Summers to come away with me alone; Sasha will be coming with us, and I thought a member of your department could accompany us too. Doležal also has some Roman artefacts I am interested in and I thought Dr Matherson could help me out there.'

'Count me in!' said Luke with enthusiasm. 'I've always wanted to see the Charles Bridge.'

Elfie was embarrassed about the fact that all her colleague was interested in was having a good time on this man's money. However, she still felt cross that she seemed to have no say in the matter. 'I don't know . . . ' she said again, unable to articulate her discomfort.

David cleared his throat. 'Mr Carter has given the University a substantial donation to compensate for your time, Elfie.'

So, Gabriel had bought her. She wanted to scream at him but, unbidden and unexpected, the memory of his hand warm in her own flashed into her mind, along with his compliment, *you really are amazing*. Angrily she shook her head. 'All right, I'll go.'

David beamed. 'So that's settled.'

They all stood up and Gabriel shook their hands. 'I'll pick you up at midday tomorrow. I have your addresses.'

'I look forward to it,' said Luke and he exited quickly, eager to start preparing for the trip.

Elfie left the office close behind, but stopped when she felt a touch on her arm. She turned around and glared at Gabriel, shaking off his hand. 'What?' she snapped.

He laughed. 'That's hardly the way to speak to someone who's invited you on a free weekend in Prague.'

She took a step closer to him and poked him in the chest. 'Now you understand this. I'm doing it for the University, not for you. Money doesn't impress me, Mr Carter, and flashing it around most certainly doesn't. I really object to being made to feel that I haven't been given the choice.'

Gabriel stared at her. 'If you really don't want to go, then don't. David can keep the cheque. I really don't want you to feel that you've been coerced into this trip. I honestly thought you'd enjoy it.'

'Oh, very clever,' Elfie retorted. 'Now I'm being stupid, pedantic and childish if I say no.'

He held up his hands. 'Is there any way I can come out of this conversation without feeling like the bad guy?'

She took off her glasses and massaged the bridge of her nose with her thumb and forefinger. 'Mr Carter — '

'Gabriel, please.'

She ignored him. 'I'll be ready tomorrow, I'll come with you and I'll verify the Buckle, if it's there. Other than that, don't expect too much from me.'

'Okay.' He watched her replace her

glasses and gave her a soft smile. 'I'll see you tomorrow, then.'

She watched him walk back into David's office and then went into her own room. She sat there for a while, mulling over his words. Although the way she had been manipulated still rankled, she was unable to suppress a rising feeling of excitement.

She was going to Prague, and it was possible that she might see the Buckle of Bohemia, which she had read about since she was a child. It would be like finding Excalibur, or the Holy Grail!

She thought about the legend, about the fact that if you touched the Buckle, it would allegedly bring you true love. True love would be at the very bottom of her Christmas wish list. There was no way that Elfie was going to allow herself to fall in love and become vulnerable to anyone, let alone a flashy businessman who could have any woman he wanted at the drop of a hat, and was probably about as reliable as the English train service.

Still, if the Buckle actually was in Prague, perhaps she should steer clear of coming into contact with it.

Especially if Gabriel Carter was around.

2

The next day, there was a knock on the door of Elfie's flat at twelve o'clock sharp. 'Come in!' she called.

'I could have been anyone,' Gabriel admonished as he entered. Elfie looked up from her packing. He wore a casual light green sweater and jeans with a long, black, heavy woollen coat and looked, quite honestly, gorgeous. She watched him look around the room in shock. 'Good grief! What have you done, raided the British Library? There must be more books in here than all the Waterstones in England!'

She followed his gaze. Her books had quickly outgrown the few shelves in her tiny flat and they now covered so much of the floor she could barely see the carpet.

'I like reading,' she said defensively.

'So I see.'

She ran her hand over the satin surface of the nearest tome. 'I enjoy holding them as much as reading them.'

'Would you two like to be alone?'

She flushed. 'There's no need to make fun of me.'

He held up his hands. 'I wouldn't dream of it. I would have bought more over the years too, but my wife said they just collected dust.' His eyes darkened with memories, like a cloud passing over the sun.

'Your wife?' Her heart stumbled in its rhythm. How stupid! Of course a handsome man like Gabriel was going to be married.

He brushed an ancient, dusty book on Stonehenge with his hand. His head was bent and she couldn't see his face. 'My late wife. She died eighteen months ago, of breast cancer.'

'Oh, I'm sorry,' she said, meaning it, and thinking how awful to lose a partner at such a young age. And of course, that was probably why he was opening the museum and giving the proceeds to a cancer charity. Perhaps he was even going to dedicate it to his wife, she thought.

She saw that he was touched by her sincerity. 'It was a release,' he admitted. 'For both of us.' He cleared his throat. 'Let's not talk about it now. We've got a weekend in the most beautiful city in the world; let's make the most of it!'

'I'm all packed,' she said, indicating her case. 'I was just trying to decide which books to take.'

'Well it's not as if you're stuck for choice.' He grinned. 'I wouldn't worry, I don't think you'll have time for reading.'

'I'm not a great television watcher, Mr Carter. I'd be lost without a book in the evenings.'

He laughed. 'Do you really think I'll whisk you away only to let you stay in all night? I know how to show a girl a good time!' He winked at her, then laughed. 'Don't blush! Look, I know you don't like money being flashed about, but I'll be discreet. And will you please call me Gabriel?'

She said nothing. Calling him Mr Carter reminded her that this was purely a business trip and that he was a private collector. Calling him Gabriel felt too familiar for her liking.

'Have you got a lot of money?' she asked, deliberately reminding herself why she disliked him.

'Subtle's not exactly your middle name, is it?'

'I like to know these things.'

'You might turn into a fortune hunter if I tell you.'

'That,' she said, 'is never going to happen.'

'Oh, you say that now, but you'd be surprised how money can turn a girl's head,' he teased.

Her lips twitched. 'Why won't you tell me?'

'I don't know.'

She frowned. 'You don't know why you won't tell me?'

He sighed. 'I meant that I don't know how much I'm worth.'

'What do you mean? I know how much money I have to the nearest penny! You must have an idea.'

'I honestly don't know; I don't sit counting it every day. Somewhere between fifteen and twenty million, I suppose.' He began to laugh at the look on her face. 'What?'

'Good grief, I had no idea . . . '

'Is it a problem?'

She shrugged. 'Did you make it all selling artefacts?'

'Look, Miss-Hundred-and-One-Questions, let's get going and I'll answer everything you want to know en route.' He indicated the thin sweater she was wearing. 'Will you be warm enough in that? It'll be colder in Prague.'

'I'm putting this on over the top.' She pulled on a brightly coloured, oversized jumper without removing her glasses. Then she remembered she had them on when the neck of the jumper wouldn't go over her head.

'Here,' she heard him say as he came forward and lifted the edge of the jumper and carefully slid her glasses off her nose. She pulled the rest of the jumper down, blushing furiously at his intimate gesture.

When her head was through, she saw him looking through the glasses. 'Do you have to wear these all the time?' he frowned. 'They're a very weak prescription, aren't they?'

'What are you implying?'

'Nothing. Come on, let's get going. Luke will be waiting.' He tried to take her bag from her hand.

She gripped it tightly. 'It's okay.'

'No, let me . . . '

'It's alright, I can manage.'

'I know that, for God's sake! It's called good manners!'

She let go, flustered, locking her door and following him down the stairs. Outside on the street sat a silver Aston Martin, sleek as a giant cat. She stopped and stared.

He grinned proudly, opening the boot and putting her bag in. 'I know, gorgeous isn't it?'

She nodded, impressed. With all his money he could so easily have chosen something red and flashy. But this was elegant and sophisticated. Very Gabriel, she decided.

He opened the door for her, holding up a hand as she went to protest. 'You'll have to get off your feminist high horse this weekend. I — can't stop being a gentleman just because you're uncomfortable with it.'

It's not that, she protested silently as she slid into the Aston. I'm just not used to it.

He walked around the car to the other side, got in and started the engine. It purred like the great cat it resembled. She felt acutely aware of how near they were sitting. His left leg was very close to her right. She found her eyes drawn to the way his jeans stretched across his thigh. He looked over his shoulder to reverse and caught her eye. He smiled and she looked away, embarrassed that he had seen her staring at him.

She needed a few moments to think clearly, but it was hard with him so near. It was difficult to breathe, as if all the oxygen had been sucked out of the car. She was conscious of the subtle smell of his aftershave, mingled with that of the leather seats. It was such a masculine atmosphere.

'So you were going to tell me how you made all your money,' she said, trying to distract herself.

'Ah yes, the money. Well I'm afraid it's not as interesting as collecting arte-facts. I discovered when I was young that I had a talent for technology. When I was twenty-two, I invented a desktop publishing program that was better than anything else on the market at the time. I opened my own company, and here we are. It's all very boring really.'

'Hmm.' Despite herself, she was im-pressed. 'I suppose at least your business ventures mean you've got plenty of cash to buy nice trinkets,' she said, a slight dig at his treasure hunting.

'I guess,' he replied, giving her a

sideways glance. He was quiet for a moment. Then he said out of the blue, 'So you're not living with anyone?'

She realised that although she didn't wear a wedding band, he hadn't known if she was attached until he saw her flat. 'No,' she confirmed. She looked out of the side window at the Edwardian houses flashing by. 'And not likely to be, either.'

'Oh?'

'Let's just say that I'm married to my work.'

'Like Queen Elizabeth the First?'

She glared at him. 'Don't you start!'

He grinned. 'Did you and Luke have something going once?'

'Not in the least! I detest the man! And now I have to put up with both of you for an entire weekend!'

'Oh, that wasn't my fault,' he said. 'David told me he wouldn't let you go unless someone else in the department went as a chaperone.'

'Really?' She was puzzled. 'I wonder why . . . '

'I've no idea.' His eyes danced again, suggesting he was about to tease her. 'Perhaps he was worried that I might seduce you.'

She couldn't stop a blush spreading to her cheeks. 'I don't understand,' she blurted out, angry now at his playfulness. 'Why do you keep saying these things? I find it quite hurtful.'

'Hurtful? Good grief, why?'

'Just stop pretending that you find me attractive.'

He gave her a puzzled look. 'You're joking, right?'

'Gabriel, I'm not stupid, I know you're making fun of me. Do I look like the sort of woman that men can't keep their hands off of?'

He stared at her for so long that she began to worry he would crash the car. Finally he looked back at the road. 'Luke wanted to date you.'

'He likes a challenge, that's all. He wanted to break me in, like a horse.'

His eyes took on a flinty gleam. 'Do you think I'm the same? That I'm only interested in the chase?'

She felt her cheeks grow hot again. 'I have no idea. I'm just saying that, like Luke, I'm sure you have no trouble in attracting beautiful women, and I know he only thought of me as a challenge and would have dumped me as soon as I gave in. So don't insult me with these flippant compliments, because I'm not interested in having a relationship with anyone, however hard they try.' She finished breathless and with a quiver in her voice.

'Has it ever occurred to you that Luke genuinely fancied you? That he sincerely wanted to date you?'

'No. Because he didn't. I'd bet my flat on it.'

He gave her his fond, slightly puzzled smile that she was beginning to wonder if he reserved just for her. 'I think,' he said, 'that you've been acting Plain Jane for so long that you actually think you've turned into her.' He pulled the car over. 'Here's Luke's house,' he said. 'Wait here.'

She sat there as he got out, stunned. She had known him for just over twenty-four hours, and he already seemed to understand her more than anyone she had ever known. It was the first time that a man had seen through her 'disguise'. She deliberately hid behind her professorial image, and usually it worked. Apart from Luke, men paid her very little attention, and she was completely happy with that.

Wasn't she? She had to admit to herself that a small part of her did enjoy the way Gabriel was flirting with her. But she had been hurt in the past, she reminded herself, and she wasn't going to let herself be vulnerable again.

The two men returned to the car. Luke jumped in the back behind her.

'Morning Queenie.'

'Morning Jackass.'

'What a nice, friendly trip this is going to be.' Gabriel got in and started the engine. 'Try and be civil you two, for sanity's sake.' He pulled away and took the road out of town.

'Where's Sasha meeting us?' Elfie asked.

'At Exeter Airport. We were staying in a hotel nearby so she's getting a taxi.' He glanced across at her. 'Separate rooms, before you say anything, Miss Nosey Parker.'

She shot him a cross look. She had indeed wondered if they were an item and felt irritated at herself for the surge of pleasure she felt when he confirmed that they weren't.

'What time's our flight?' Luke asked.

Gabriel gave him an amused grin in the rear-view mirror and said, 'Whenever we get there.'

Elfie stared at him. 'Oh, don't tell me you have a private jet?'

'I apologise if that appears flashy but it's simply convenient; I spend more time in the air than I do on the ground most weeks.' He shrugged. 'I can book us a chartered flight if you like but you might have to wait a few days.'

'Wow,' said Luke. 'Is it big?'

'It's not Air Force One or anything, if that's what you mean.'

She felt excited, in spite of her feelings towards Gabriel and Luke. This was turning out to be quite a weekend!

'Have you been to Prague before?' she asked Gabriel as he wound the car through the busy Topsham streets.

'On many occasions.' After a pause, he added, 'My wife came from the Czech Republic.' Again he sounded tense. He must have loved her very much, Elfie thought.

'You're married?' Luke asked.

'Was. She died.'

'What was her name?' said Elfie, intrigued in spite of herself.

'Juliet Kopřiva. Her father was Czech but her mother was English.'

Elfie looked out of the window, seeing the Christmas trees in the houses as they drove slowly by. She had heard that Eastern European women were generally very beautiful, and wondered if this had been the case with Gabriel's wife.

'Have either of you been to Prague?' he asked.

'No,' said Luke, 'but I've always wanted to.'

Elfie shook her head. 'I haven't travelled much at all. But I have read about it, and I am looking forward to going.'

Gabriel smiled. 'It's very beautiful at this time of year. I'd love you to see it when it snows.' He sounded eager, which puzzled her. Why should he care what she thought of the city?

He turned off towards the airport and parked the car, then they made their way into the airport lounge. Sasha was waiting and they went immediately to the terminal. Elfie was impressed; the only time she had flown had been on a short flight to France, and that had been in the summer, when the plane was delayed for two hours and the lounge was choc-a-bloc with people. This was much nicer!

She walked across the runway with Sasha, who had dressed down compared to the day before and was wearing casual grey wool trousers and a blue jumper over a white shirt — although her hair and make-up were still perfectly immaculate.

'Do you fly with Mr Carter often?' Elfie asked politely.

'Oh yes, Gabe takes me everywhere,' Sasha replied in her upper-class English accent, making Elfie aware of her own Devon burr. 'He'd be lost without me.' She leaned closer conspiratorially. 'I don't think he'd even be able to get dressed if I wasn't there to organise him!'

Elfie doubted that that was the case, but recognised the undercurrent beneath the words: she had just been warned off. Sasha obviously saw herself as a replacement for the deceased Mrs Carter. Was that Gabriel's plan too, she wondered?

Ahead of them was a small but beautiful aircraft, of which Gabriel was obviously very proud, judging by the way he ran his hand along it. She followed him on board. Inside was a small office, and behind that a lounge with two leather sofas facing each other.

Behind this were several chairs with seatbelts. She sat in one of the seats and buckled herself in, and the others did the same. The rich brown carpet and cream decor were elegant and stylish. A young male flight attendant closed the doors and checked their belts before speaking to the pilot.

It wasn't long before the plane taxied down the runway. Soon they were climbing rapidly into the sky, the sun shining clearly amongst the few clouds. The attendant unclipped himself. 'You can leave your seats now,' he said. 'The flight will take about two hours, so if anyone's hungry I can prepare some lunch.'

'That will be great, Andy, thanks.' Gabriel directed them all to the sofas. Sasha sat and Luke took the seat next to her and Gabriel sat beside Elfie.

'The weather's fine so it should be a calm flight. Can you bring some sandwiches please, Andy?'

Andy nodded, disappearing through the curtains at the back of the plane.

'Can you brief us on our schedule?' asked Luke.

'Of course,' said Gabriel. 'I've arranged to meet Doležal tomorrow at eleven. In the afternoon I'm afraid I have another meeting to go to, but it will give you some time to relax as you wish. I thought we might go to the opera on Saturday evening.'

'That would be wonderful,' Elfie exclaimed. The opera! Luke pulled a face, but the idea appealed to her greatly.

'What about tonight?' Luke asked.

'Just dinner. There's a lovely restaurant in our hotel.'

'Oh, it's a long time since I've been to an expensive restaurant.' The words were out of Elfie's mouth before she could stop them. Immediately she regretted it; Luke rolled his eyes and whispered something to Sasha, who giggled. Elfie flushed.

Gabriel ignored them and turned to her. 'I didn't say anything about it being expensive,' he said softly so the other two couldn't hear. 'I thought you didn't like a man to throw his money around?'

'I just can't imagine you in a burger bar,' she said truthfully. She felt a surge of gratitude for his good manners; by speaking quietly he had excluded the other two from their conversation, showing her that he disapproved of their behaviour.

'I'm rather partial to Big Macs, actually.'

She laughed. 'The thought of you sitting at a plastic table surrounded by children and Happy Meals is quite a picture!'

'Well I hope that will happen one day.'

She considered him for a moment. 'You want children?'

'Doesn't everyone?' He studied her thoughtfully. 'Don't you?'

'I don't know,' she admitted, flustered. 'I suppose it's something I always thought I'd do one day, like learning Italian.'

'It's kind of difficult for them to come about if you're determined to be 'married to your work'.'

'I suppose. I really haven't given it much thought.' It was true. She had no desire to engage in a relationship, but suddenly the thought that she might never have children brought a lump to her throat. What was it about this man that enabled him to touch such sensitive parts of her soul when she had known him for so little time?

To her relief, at that moment Andy came out with the sandwiches. She buried her head in a Prague guide book for the rest of the flight while Gabriel made business calls and Sasha and Luke chatted. It seemed like no time at all before Andy was informing them that they would be touching down at Ruzyně Airport shortly and would they all take their seats and buckle up.

Elfie did so, beginning to feel nervous about the weekend. It was purely business, she told herself firmly. She would meet Doležal, have a look at the Buckle — which was only a piece of metal and had no magical powers whatsoever — and return home again. She would ignore Gabriel's attempts to try and make her have fun. She would not go out, she would not dine with him, nor accompany him to the opera. This was purely business.

She gulped as the plane's wheels landed on the runway with a slight bounce. Who was she kidding? This was probably going to be the hardest weekend of her life!

3

As their car travelled the short distance to the city centre, Luke asked, 'Where are we staying?'

'It's called the Ungelt.' Gabriel was sitting next to the driver and he turned in his seat to speak to the three of them in the back. 'It's a beautiful, small hotel tucked away in a quiet street behind Old Town Square.'

Elfie sighed. Gabriel seemed to be going out of his way to ensure that he did not appear flashy. Their car was an example: dark and sleek, expensive but not ostentatious. She had expected him to book into the most expensive hotel in Prague, but it sounded as if he had chosen something discreet.

Was he always this way — or was he deliberately trying to impress her? After spending so much time with Luke at work, Elfie found it difficult to believe it was anything other than the latter, knowing that if Luke had Gabriel's sort of money, he would be lounging in a pool in Hawaii with fifteen or so young women and bottles of champagne on ice.

Gabriel will slip up at some point though, she thought, and vastly over-tip a waiter or something, and then he would reveal his true nature.

'This is the Old Town,' he said as the car wound its way through the medieval streets. 'I find it fascinating because it's so different to Western Europe. Both the language and the architecture show little influence from the Romans and it just seems so un-English.'

'I know what you mean.' Elfie looked out at the churches with their seventeenth-century Baroque influence, unlike the medieval hand-me-downs of England. 'I can see why you like it so much.'

Sasha was talking quietly to Luke about something unrelated to the scenery and Elfie got the impression that the woman was trying to appear nonchalant about

43

the city, making it clear that she had been there many times. She sighed and looked out of the window again. Visiting a foreign city was a real experience for her and she wasn't going to let Sasha spoil it.

After a few more minutes the car pulled up outside a small hotel and Gabriel got out, opening the door for Elfie. Together they made their way up the stairs into the lobby, where Gabriel went to the desk to check them in and request the keys for their rooms.

'I'm surprised at him,' Luke whispered to Elfie. 'I thought with all his dough he might have chosen somewhere a bit more impressive.'

'I think it's lovely,' she said sincerely, recognising the sophistication in the marble floors, expensive rugs and stylish wooden furniture. 'Not everyone likes to splash money around like you do.'

He looked at her, amused. 'Are you defending him?' He raised his eyebrows as she blushed. 'Don't tell me someone's actually found a way beneath

Queen Elizabeth's skin?'

'I don't know what you're talking about,' she said sharply. 'I detest private collectors, you know that.'

'Hmm.' He seemed unconvinced. He looked disgruntled and she had the impression that he was angry at the idea that some other man had been able to crack her when he had not.

She turned away and accepted her keycard from Gabriel, looking forward to spending a while alone. The porters took them in a lift to their rooms, and Elfie let herself into her suite.

She gasped appreciatively when she stepped inside. The room was spacious and airy, painted in a light, fresh colour. The big bed draped in a stylish quilt, and there was a small kitchenette off to one side. She walked around, investigating the tiled bathroom with its large bath and separate shower, and then looked through the window at the shady terrace and well-kept garden below.

'Is everything all right?'

She turned from the window to see

Gabriel tipping the porter discreetly. The man nodded his thanks and withdrew. So much for her theory of him being ostentatious with his money!

'It's beautiful,' she admitted. 'But I can't accept such a luxurious suite, Mr Carter. I would have been quite happy with a small room.'

He grinned. 'Your colleague didn't seem to have any trouble accepting it! Although I'm sure he would have preferred the Ritz.'

She realised that he must have overheard Luke's earlier comments about the hotel and felt embarrassed. 'I'm sorry about him, he — '

'Don't apologise for him; he doesn't deserve your defence.' Gabriel's voice was sharp. Then he softened it to add, 'And I wouldn't dream of you taking a smaller room; it's the least I can do after you've dropped everything to come with me. Now, it's half past three. I've taken the liberty of booking a table in the restaurant here for eight o'clock — I hope that's all right for you?'

She remembered her silent vow in the car to refuse to dine with him, but found that she couldn't say no when he asked her so nicely. She was also determined to be pleasant after Luke's rudeness, not wanting him to go away with the wrong idea about the University. 'That would be lovely.'

'Great. Well after you've had a rest, perhaps you would like a short walk around the town?'

She thought about it. What harm could come from taking in the sights? With Luke and Sasha present, hopefully there wouldn't be too much personal conversation. 'Okay, that would be nice.'

'Good. I'll meet you in the lobby in an hour.'

He left, shutting the door quietly behind him. Elfie sighed again. So much for the vows she had made to herself in the car! But she wasn't going to berate herself too much. The city was too beautiful and she was too excited to be there to be ungracious.

She made herself a cup of coffee

47

in the kitchenette, pulled a book from her bag and lay on the bed to read. A pleasant way to spend any spare hour!

★ ★ ★

Later she pulled on her large jacket and donned a woolly hat and gloves, determined not to get frostbite during their walk. She came down the stairs, seeing Gabriel standing in front of the desk. He was wearing his black overcoat and held gloves in his hand. As she walked up to him, he grinned at her woolly hat.

'Where are the other two?' she asked.

'I've no idea.'

She stared at him. Clearly he hadn't asked them to accompany them on their walk. 'Perhaps I should go and see if they want to come . . . '

He raised an eyebrow. 'Do you really want to do that?'

She couldn't stop her smile. 'No, not really.'

'Well come on, then.' He winked at her.

Heart thumping, she followed him out the front door, the air cold on her face. He pulled on his gloves, his breath frosting before him. 'I thought we'd just have a meander around Old Town Square and then maybe walk over the Charles Bridge — it's not far.'

'Okay.' She felt surprisingly happy as they began to walk down the Stupartská road, flanked by houses and shops with beautiful Baroque and Renaissance façades. She pointed up at a pair of steeples that rose above the surrounding houses. 'What do they belong to?'

'The Church of Our Lady before Týn,' he said. 'It's the Old Town's most distinctive landmark.'

'It's like something out of Sleeping Beauty,' she remarked.

'The whole city looks like the setting of a Disney cartoon.'

She glanced at him. He was obviously fond of the place. 'You must have many happy memories of being here,' she said.

He looked across and she was

surprised to see his eyes so dark. 'Some,' was all he said, but even in the twenty-four hours that she had known him, Elfie recognised that he was lying, that he had painful memories rather than pleasant ones.

'Here's the Old Town Square,' he said as they emerged from a side road into the open space of the old marketplace.

Elfie gasped. 'Oh, it's beautiful.'

'I knew you'd like it,' he said, pleased. 'Come on, let's walk around and I'll tell you what I know.'

They toured the four sides of the square, then wandered along the streets towards the river. 'The Charles Bridge is supposed to be one of the most romantic places in the world. More people are said to propose there than anywhere else in Europe,' he told her.

'Did you propose to Juliet there?' she asked curiously.

Once again his eyes darkened. 'Actually no, we were in London at the time.' He didn't seem to want to talk about her, and Elfie decided to ask him no more questions, not wanting to make him unhappy.

They came to the Old Town Bridge Tower and emerged through it onto the Bridge itself. Flanked by many statues, it spanned the width of the River Vltava in a series of arches. All the way along were craft and trinket stalls, and in the middle a man dressed in a tuxedo was singing a love song along to a cassette playing music.

'I can see why it got its reputation,' she admitted. 'It's very romantic.' They walked across the road and she leaned on the wall, overlooking the river. Gabriel joined her, his arm not quite touching hers, but she was sure she could almost feel the heat of his body, even through their layers of thick winter clothing.

'Are any of these statues of Princess Libuse with whom Charlemagne fell in love?' she asked, trying to concentrate on why they were in Prague.

'Not here, but there's an Art

Nouveau statue in Charles Street — I can show you on the way back, if you like.' He looked across at her. 'Charlemagne must have loved her very much, to give her such a treasured heirloom, don't you think?'

'I suppose.'

'You still find it difficult to believe that a man would love a woman so much he would do anything to make her happy?'

She shrugged. 'Well, yes. In the real world. I don't believe in a love so strong that it blinds you to all reason.'

He studied her for a moment, then turned back to the river. 'So tell me why you're so convinced that you're married to your work,' he asked quietly.

This was just what she didn't want; personal conversation. 'I don't know what you mean. I love my job, archaeology is everything to me. I can't imagine being involved in anything else.'

'I understand that. Your reputation precedes you. It's well known that you're the authority on Anglo-Saxon jewellery.' He gave the compliment easily, just a throwaway statement, but still, she felt her cheeks glow with the accolade. 'But that's not what I meant,' he continued, 'and I think you know that. Of course you should never be expected to give up your career for love. But the two aren't mutually exclusive. However, you seemed convinced — determined, even — that you won't find anyone with whom you'll feel comfortable enough to settle down. And I just wondered why that was.'

She leaned over the bridge and watched the boats passing under the arches. She didn't want him to see her face, to see her vulnerability, her confusion. Just how did this man have the ability to coax out her secrets, like other men wheedled whelks out of their shells?

She said nothing for a moment, uncomfortable with the fact that she couldn't formulate an argument. She knew that whatever line of reasoning she came up with, he would have an answer which would appear much more logical and would only serve to confuse her more.

Eventually, aware that he was watching her patiently, she faced him. 'I'm not ready to share that with you,' she admitted. 'I've only known you for a day, and I'm only here for a weekend on a business trip. I don't really think you can ask me to divulge that sort of information.'

'It sounds like I'm asking for the codes to arm a missile,' he replied with amusement, but he didn't press her. 'I know it's only been twenty-four hours, but it seems like longer.'

She knew what he meant. How strange to think that he had only come into her life yesterday and yet he already seemed to understand her so well.

He touched her briefly on the arm. 'I'm sorry to have pried into what is obviously your very private life, Elfie. I meant no harm. I just find it very sad to think that such a lovely young woman has closed her heart to love and I wanted to understand why. I like you, and I hope that if nothing else, we can become friends. Then perhaps one day you will feel able to explain it all.'

He sounded very sincere, as if he truly cared about her. For some bizarre reason, she felt her eyes fill with tears and she looked away across the water, biting her lip.

She had friends, of course, three or four, all female, that she met up with occasionally for coffee or lunch, and other colleagues and acquaintances that she saw from time to time. But since the death of her parents there had been no one that she had become close to, no one that had shown as much interest in her wellbeing as this man that she had only just met.

Experience had taught her that you can't trust men — and you can't trust love. She wasn't going to let go of that overnight. But some part of her, the seed of her sensitivity that had until now been frozen inside her heart, thawed just a little.

'Perhaps we should go back,' she said quietly. 'It's been a busy, tiring day and I think I'd like to have a short rest before dinner, if that's alright.'

'Of course.' He was the perfect gentleman again, and refrained from discussing anything personal as they left the bridge behind, much to her relief. When they passed through Charles Street, he showed her the statue of the Princess Libuse and Elfie studied her solemnly, wondering at the passion between her and Charlemagne that had caused him to give her — as Gabriel had said — a treasured heirloom.

They walked back to the hotel in companionable silence and Gabriel reminded her that dinner was at eight, before disappearing into his suite. Elfie let herself into her own rooms, running a hot bath and eventually sliding into the bubbles until she was up to her neck in suds. She found it hard to relax, though, because she kept thinking about all the issues that Gabriel's questions were stirring up inside her.

She knew she had never been in love. Of course, that was what she had always wanted, what she had avoided at all costs, but now, for some reason, she couldn't stop herself wondering what such overwhelming passion would feel like.

She wondered if Gabriel had had that sort of relationship with his wife. It didn't sound like it had been a marriage of convenience, so presumably they must have been close at some point. The thought of him being in love with someone else left a strange, tight feeling around her throat.

His words on the Bridge had unlocked the solid cage that she had placed around her heart and all sorts of feelings had come flooding out. Her promise to herself over ten years ago to never open herself up to being hurt seemed childish all of a sudden. It had been an easy promise to keep for so long, she realised, because she had never met a man that she had liked anywhere near enough to break it.

She thought about how it would feel to be married, to be coming home every night to someone like Gabriel. To . . . oh, my God, to be going to bed every night with him too. She felt her cheeks flame and sank a little further into the bath.

Sex was a word that she had totally omitted from her vocabulary. She had never admitted to her female friends that she was still a virgin, and she joined in with their sometimes bawdy jokes, pretending that she knew what they were talking about. But basically she didn't have a clue.

She knew how unusual she was in this day and age — twenty five, and still hadn't slept with a man. But she had never really given it much thought. The thought of undressing in front of a man, of letting him . . . She shook her head. It wasn't something she had ever thought about, not with film stars, not with Luke nor with any other man she had met.

Even when she was younger, any time she had begun to wonder what sex or even kissing was like, she had opened a book and stuck her nose in it and read until the thought had gone out of her head. Having sex had never seemed like a thing she could conceive of wanting to do, ever.

Until now.

For the first time in her life, Elfie imagined what it would be like to be kissed. She closed her eyes and pictured Gabriel's face, the softness of his newly-shaven skin, or maybe with a hint of stubble, his deep brown eyes with that hint of a smile in them, his dark hair thick between her fingers. She thought how it would feel to have his lips touch hers as he wrapped his arms around her . . .

Oh, goodness gracious, what was she doing? Did she have a fever? Was she ill? She had just met the man and here she was imagining all sorts of things about him!

She didn't want a man, she reminded herself fiercely. Men were trouble, you couldn't trust them, and they let you down. They hurt you, and she was never going to let herself be hurt again.

Crossly she leaned over the bath and picked up the Archaeology magazine that was lying on the floor. Opening it at the beginning, she made herself read about the latest developments in carbon dating. If anything would get thoughts of love out of her head, it would be this!

4

Just before eight o'clock that evening, she left her room in a slightly calmer frame of mind. As she descended the stairs, however, and saw Gabriel standing with Luke at the bottom in the lobby, she felt her knees go a bit wobbly. Would he somehow be able to tell what she had imagined in her room? However, as she walked up to them, Gabriel just gave her a gentle smile, and complimented her on the way she looked.

Seeing how they were both dressed, however, she realised that his compliment must be merely polite, her thought confirmed by the slight sneer on Luke's face as he looked her up and down. The men were both wearing suits and ties, and she suddenly wished she had brought something smarter with her. The problem was that she didn't own anything dressy. She was wearing soft black trousers and shoes with a low heel, a plain cream jumper and pearls that had belonged to her mother. Her hair was scraped back in its usual ponytail, although she had washed it, aware that it gleamed like polished copper before she tied it up.

Suddenly she worried about what Sasha was going to appear in. Her worst fears were realised as she saw the PA descending, looking like a model who had stepped straight off the cat-walk. Sasha was wearing a deep red dress that clung to her curves, making Elfie vividly aware of her own rather boyish figure. The PA's black hair hung loose across her shoulders like a satin sheet, and she wore glorious high heels the exact same shade as her dress, which emphasised her long legs to perfection.

Elfie felt like her dowdy country cousin. She wondered why it bothered her. Normally she never gave more than a couple of seconds' thought to her outfit. She knew the answer, however, as Gabriel complimented Sasha on her appearance. He used exactly the same words that he had said to Elfie as she had come down, but somehow she was certain that this time they were more sincere.

However as they turned to go into the dining room, it was to her that he turned and offered his arm, and she took it with a smile, thinking what an old fashioned gesture it was, but recognising that he was being considerate of her feelings. She walked with him down the steps, thinking how charming the restaurant was. As in the lobby, the floors were marble and the furniture was elegant without being ostentatious. Nearly all the tables were full, and she realised that it must be a very exclusive place to eat.

They were shown to a table near the large windows that looked out over the gardens, and Elfie took a seat that the waiter pulled out for her. Gabriel sat opposite her and Luke beside her, with Sasha taking the final seat next to Gabriel. Elfie wondered what they looked like to other people, who might assume they were there on pleasure rather than business. Did it look as if she were partnered with Luke, or Gabriel? They were both good-looking men. But instinctively she knew whom she would choose.

As if he could read her thoughts, Gabriel met her gaze and he smiled. She flushed and lifted the menu to hide her face. For goodness' sake, she thought, let me get through this evening without blushing all night!

The menu was simple and international and Elfie chose a vegetable soup followed by a pasta dish. The meal progressed without incident, accompanied by light conversation about a variety of subjects. Elfie purposely remained quiet, concentrating on her food and on not letting her feet bump into Gabriel's under the table.

It was only when it was time to order the dessert that all four of them seemed to relax a little.

'I can recommend the fruit dumplings,'

Gabriel said. 'They're a Czech speciality; you can't go home without trying them.'

'Then dumplings it will be,' said Elfie, noting that they were served with melted butter, icing sugar and ground poppy seeds. She saw that Sasha declined a dessert and realised that the woman had actually eaten very little all evening. That was presumably how she retained her svelte figure.

Even as the thought passed through her head, Sasha looked over at Elfie, seemingly disgruntled. 'I don't know how you can put such rubbish into your body,' she commented. 'It will go straight to your hips.'

'Sasha!' Gabriel shot her an angry glance. 'That was rude.'

Elfie shook her head at him. 'I think the dumplings will have trouble finding my hips,' she said wryly, aware that she did not have the most curvaceous figure. 'It's not a habit of mine to eat like this,' she told the PA.

'So you do diet?' Sasha stated with satisfaction.

'Oh, God no. I just hate cooking. I live on microwave meals, if I can be bothered at all.' Elfie's voice trailed off and she realised that Sasha had probably never even seen a ready-made lasagne. She toyed with her beer, which Gabriel had ordered for her insisting that it was better than most of the wine in Prague.

Gabriel indicated Elfie's nearly full bottle. 'You don't like it?'

She shrugged. 'I don't drink much at all, really, just a sherry at Christmas.' As she said it, she saw Luke and Sasha exchange a glance and bite their lips to hide a smile. Her cheeks flushed again. Why did she keep making a fool of herself like this?

'Perhaps you would like a liqueur then?' Gabriel offered. He signalled a waiter and asked for a Slivovice.

'What's that?'

'A plum brandy. It's . . . an acquired taste, shall we say, but you might prefer it to the Pils.'

The waiter brought over a surprisingly large glass of the dark liquid. She sipped it. It was clear and sweet and clearly very strong, but much better than the beer. 'Thank you.'

'You're welcome.'

She lowered her eyes from his warm gaze, concentrating on her dessert. It was delicious; the melted butter made it a very rich dish, but it went perfectly with the liqueur. She soon finished the first drink.

Gabriel asked her if she wanted another. 'It's very strong,' he warned.

'I'm hardly drunk.'

'I wasn't criticising, just informing you.'

It seemed like no time at all before she had finished another glass, and she suddenly realised that things were getting a little hazy. 'You're right, this stuff is strong,' she observed, looking at the empty glass reluctantly. Gabriel signalled for it to be refilled and she protested, but let them do it anyway.

She looked over at the pianist playing in the corner of the room. It was some classical piece that she didn't recognise, but it was played so expertly that it gave her the shivers.

'Would you like to dance?'

She looked around in surprise as Luke asked the question, only to find that he was speaking to Sasha, not to her. The other woman smiled at him and rose elegantly, taking his hand as he led her to the small dance floor.

Elfie dropped her gaze and fiddled with her glass.

Gabriel sat back in his seat, seemingly unconcerned that the other two had left the table, but watching her, as he seemed to do a lot. He had loosened his tie a little. She saw that he was wearing elegant silver cufflinks.

'Are you feeling all right?' he asked.

'Of course. Why?'

'Just wondered.

She knew that she was slightly drunk, but didn't want to admit it. She sipped a bit more of the brandy to give herself something to do but then put the glass down, realising that that probably wasn't a good idea.

He smiled, his eyes crinkling at the edges, looking at her as if he really, honestly, liked her.

Suddenly she wanted to talk, to lighten the load lying on her heart. 'I'll tell you now,' she said.

'Tell me what?' he replied, amused.

'Why I'm determined to stay single.'

'Oh?' Suddenly he seemed very alert.

She took a long, slow, deep breath. 'When I was fifteen, my father died in a car crash.'

'Oh, I'm sorry.'

'It was quick — they said he wouldn't have felt much. Anyway, at the funeral, a strange woman came up to me and my mother.' She swallowed at the memory. 'She was very bitter, told us that my dad had been having an affair with her, and that he had been about to leave us for her when he died.'

His brow furrowed with concern. 'That must have been a real shock.'

'You could say that.'

'What happened?' he prompted her gently.

'After the funeral I took mum home. She said she wanted to sleep, that she was tired. I went out with some friends, I needed to relax.' She drained the last bit of brandy from the glass. 'While I was out, she took an overdose of sleeping tablets. I came back and saw the bottle but thought she'd had just one of them — I thought she was asleep. When I went into her room the next day I realised she was never going to wake up.'

'Oh, Elfie.' He leaned forward and took her hand. 'How terrible for you.'

Her eyes filled with tears. 'It was awful. How could my dad have done that? I promised myself there and then that I would never let that happen to me — I would never put myself in a position where I would be so vulnerable that a man could hurt me so badly that I'd want to do that to myself.'

He stroked her hand gently as she tried to compose herself. 'It was a dreadful tragedy. And you were very young. I can understand why you reacted like that. But you must realise, Elfie, that not all men would do what your dad did. Not all men cheat on their partners. And anyway, how can you be sure that the woman was telling the truth?'

She stared at him, confused. 'Why would she lie?'

'There's any number of reasons. Perhaps she wanted an affair with him but he turned her down. Or maybe they did have an affair and he'd just ended it. But even if she had told the truth, I'm sure he would have been devastated to know how much he'd hurt both you and your mother. I'm sure he would have told you both in a much more sensitive way, to cause as least pain as possible.'

'Maybe.' She pushed the glass away. 'So there you are. Now you know.'

'Yes.' He released her hand and sat back in his chair. His eyes were guarded and for once she couldn't tell what he was thinking.

She suddenly felt very tired. She

realised that some threads of her hair had come loose and on impulse took out the scrunchie, running her fingers through her loose auburn locks. 'What time are we going to the castle tomorrow?' she asked.

He was quiet for a moment and she looked up to see him staring at her hair. His eyes slid to her face and he said: 'The meeting's booked for eleven. If we leave at ten, I think — '

'Why haven't you asked me to dance?' she said abruptly.

He stopped in mid sentence and raised an eyebrow. 'Because I was in the middle of talking . . . '

'Why hadn't you asked me before that?'

'Because I knew you would say no.'

'How do you know until you ask?'

He turned the bottle of beer in front of him slowly, then looked over his shoulder to the dance floor. There were a few couples on it and the lights were dimmed, giving it a romantic air. He looked back at her, amused now. 'Dr

Summers, would you like to dance?'

'Yes.' She said it before she could think better of it.

'Okay . . . ' He put down his napkin, slid his chair back and took her hand, heading towards the small area where the other couples were moving to the music. She followed him, conscious of his warm skin against hers, and let him turn her gently so that she faced him. He slipped his right hand around her waist, took her other hand in his and they began to move to the music.

'Are you happy now?' he teased.

Suddenly she felt awkward. 'I'm sorry, I suppose you didn't want to dance, I didn't mean to make you feel like you had to . . . '

'Relax, Elfie. I would have asked an hour ago anyway but I honestly thought you'd say no.'

'I probably would have,' she admitted.

'So you're only here because you're drunk?'

Her head was fuzzy and she didn't

want to argue with him. 'I just felt like dancing, that's all.'

He looked at her for a moment, then just said, 'Okay.' Subtly, almost imperceptibly, he pulled her towards him, ostensibly to avoid another couple, but after they had passed he didn't release her.

She didn't complain. She felt very strange, as if all her senses had been turned to full volume. She drank so little, so infrequently, that she was really rather enjoying this feeling of abandonment, of not caring what she said or did. Some small part of her warned her to keep her wits about her, but she quashed it, too busy having a good time to listen to her conscience.

He was a very good dancer. They were really rather close now and she could smell his subtle aftershave, something musky with a hint of lemon, and she could feel the brush of his chin on her temple. Her left hand rested lightly on his upper arm, and she could feel the firmness of the muscle there beneath her fingers. His right hand was now in the small of her back, his left holding hers firmly but not tightly, and she enjoyed the feeling of being guided around the dance floor.

It wasn't very often that she didn't have to think for herself, she realised. She had made the decision to be alone so young, not realising that alone often meant lonely. She didn't admit it to herself much, but in her little flat with all her books, she was often lonely. And yet here she was, dancing with a gorgeous man in an exclusive restaurant in the middle of Prague, a man that she had told her terrible secret to, who now understood why she had made her life decision. He knew practically everything there was to know about her, and she knew so little about him. How strange life was.

Elfie wasn't into classical music, but the piece that the pianist was playing was strangely stirring — or was it the brandy? She could almost feel the rhythm repeated in the beat of her heart, and the beat of Gabriel's heart, thudding against her chest, they were so close now. She raised her head a little, feeling his lips against her hair. What was it about this place, this city? It was as if it had entranced her, put her under a spell. Was this what had happened to Charlemagne, all those years ago?

Gabriel was humming in her ear now, just singing along to the music, but his deep, rich voice seemed to reverberate right through her. The voice of an archangel, she thought with a smile. She felt strange, as if she were becoming a part of the music, of the romance of the city. Lord, that brandy must be strong, she thought, but she didn't care. She turned her head slightly so that his lips brushed her cheek. Then, before she knew what was happening, his mouth met hers.

He kissed her gently, softly, slowly. It was nothing like she had imagined in the bath earlier. Her heart hammered inside her chest but outwardly she remained calm, resigned. His mouth was extraordinarily soft, and she could taste the beer he had been drinking. Along with the smell of his aftershave, she was suddenly overwhelmed with the completely unfamiliar sheer essence of male, the slight scrape of stubble on his cheek, the feel of his hand holding hers, larger than her own. He kissed her carefully, almost awkwardly, as a photographer might capture an image of a deer, afraid that at any minute it might take flight and leave him with just a dream. But she let him, suddenly wanting it more than anything else in the world.

She felt his arm move from her waist up around her back, pulling her closer and he kissed her harder, apparently realising that it was what she wanted, too. Involuntarily her lips parted under his and she was suddenly flooded with the warmth and the heat of him. It was such a difference to his cool lips that electricity shot through her and she gasped. The slight sound brought them both to their senses as if someone had thrown a bucket of water over them.

They pulled apart sharply. She stood

there, trembling, a hand on her lips, thinking that the whole room must be staring at them, but as she cast a quick glance around she saw that those on the dance floor were absorbed in each other, and were paying no attention to what she and Gabriel were doing. Still, she remained apart from him. He stood in front of her, unsure what to say, what to do.

'I'm sorry . . . ' he said eventually, running a hand through his hair.

Why was he apologising? She knew that she had encouraged him. She had wanted him to kiss her, desperately. It wasn't his fault that she was now in complete confusion.

'I've got to go . . . ' she whispered. She made her way quickly back to the table, grabbed her bag and walked to the exit. Only there did she give a look over her shoulder. He was still standing on the dance floor, staring after her, hands on hips, oblivious to those people around him who were now casting him glances, not even seeing Sasha and

Luke still absorbed in their own dance to one side.

Fleeing the room, she ran up the stairs to her suite, hurriedly let herself in, and buried her head in the pillow.

5

The next morning, Elfie stood nervously outside the door of Gabriel's hotel room. She had had a terrible night's sleep. For several hours she had been terrified that he would come up to her room demanding to know what she thought she was doing, kissing him and then running away.

There's a name for a woman like that, she had scolded herself. Goodness me, a couple of glasses of alcohol and she had lost all her inhibitions! What must he be thinking of her?

After a while she realised he wasn't going to come barging in to her room and she got into bed, trying to ignore the pang of disappointment that she felt. The rest of the night had been spent fitfully, with numerous dreams about embarrassing situations and making a fool of herself.

When she finally awoke in the morning, she knew that she had to see him immediately to apologise for her behaviour. They were due to leave at ten o'clock for Karlstein Castle, but she couldn't wait until then; she also couldn't bring herself to eat breakfast. By nine o'clock she was showered, dressing in smart grey trousers and a white roll neck jumper, as although it wasn't cold in the room, she knew it would be outside. There was no point in putting it off any longer. If he was going to send her back to England, she would rather get it over with.

She knocked lightly on the door then, cringing, knocked a little louder. Perhaps he had already gone to breakfast? Inside, however, she heard footsteps, and then the door opened.

Gabriel was naked from the waist up, his face half covered in shaving foam, a white towel over his shoulder. Elfie stared at him, all thought of speech gone far from her head.

'Morning,' he said, smiling.

'Sorry,' she finally managed to say. 'I thought you'd be ready . . . '

'I was delayed for ages on a phone call. Come in, I won't be long.' He walked away from the door, leaving her standing in the hallway. She hesitated, watching his broad shoulders disappear into the bathroom.

'Em . . . perhaps I should come back in a few minutes . . . '

'Can't hear you!' he called.

Closing her eyes briefly, she slipped into the room and let the door shut behind her. 'I said maybe I should — '

'Elfie, come over here, I can't hear you.'

Slowly she walked towards the bathroom, seeing him at the sink, completing his shave. He scraped the razor up one cheek, then met her eyes in the mirror as he washed the blade under the water. 'Sorry about that. Couldn't hear a word.'

'Doesn't matter,' she gulped. Her eyes wouldn't behave in spite of her trying to tear them away and her gaze ran over his taught muscles and wide chest with it's light scattering of dark hair.

He met her eyes in the mirror. 'Did you want something?'

She blushed, wondering if he'd seen her admiring him. 'I just came in to apologise for last night.'

He paused for a moment, then continued to run the razor over the final bits of shaving foam. 'For what?'

'For . . . kissing you. It was a mistake, and I shouldn't have left afterwards, it was very rude, I am sorry.'

He gathered the towel in both hands to wipe his face, then turned and walked over to her. 'I'm sorry you think it was a mistake,' he said softly. He lowered the towel. 'I enjoyed it. And I don't think it was just you kissing me, either. I believe I had something to do with it.'

She looked up and felt suddenly breathless. His skin was still damp and there were droplets of water in the hollow of his throat. His brown eyes were very warm. He didn't look angry, she thought. Quite the opposite, in fact.

She swallowed. 'Still, I shouldn't have . . . '

'Neither should I.' He smiled. 'Don't worry about it; it's forgotten.' He walked over to a white shirt hanging on his cupboard door and lifted it off the hanger and slid his arms through the sleeves:

It most certainly was not forgotten, thought Elfie, but she felt a huge sense of relief that he clearly hadn't taken offence and wasn't about to put her on the first plane out of the country.

He began to talk about the weather, saying something about the fact that it was due to snow that evening. He finished dressing as he talked, buttoning up his shirt and doing his tie, slipping on his shoes. She felt very shy, watching him, but then she recalled Sasha's comments — perhaps his PA watched him get dressed all the time.

'Elfie?'

She suddenly realised he had asked her a question. She had been watching him put on his cufflinks, thinking what a masculine gesture it was, the way he flicked his wrists as he pushed the silver clasp through the buttonhole. She looked up at his face and blushed again. 'Sorry?'

'I was just wondering if you wanted to catch some breakfast?'

'Yes, sure, of course . . . ' She felt flustered and walked to the door.

He caught her hand as she passed, however, stopping her in her tracks and turning her round. 'Are you okay?'

'Yes.'

He studied her pink cheeks. 'I've embarrassed you,' he said gently. 'I'm sorry. I didn't think.'

She shook her head and turned back to the door. 'Do they do croissants here? I'm rather partial to a croissant.' She knew she was talking too fast but he didn't say anything and just followed her out, answering her questions about the breakfast as they made their way downstairs. She had to keep the conversation away from personal matters, she scolded herself. For goodness' sake, she was supposed to be here on business!

To both their surprise, neither Luke nor Sasha were in the breakfast room. Gabriel and Elfie helped themselves to a light continental breakfast — there were croissants, to her delight — and he talked a little about Karlstein Castle as they ate, and about his business, carefully steering the conversation away from anything too intimate.

Somewhat relieved, Elfie began to be puzzled as it neared ten o'clock and there was still no sign of the other two. They went back up to their rooms to collect coats and her bag and Gabriel knocked on Luke and Sasha's rooms, but received no reply.

'I told them both we would be leaving at ten,' Gabriel said, pulling on his big black coat. He took out his phone and pressed a quick dial button, holding it to his ear.

'I'm very sorry,' Elfie said, tugging on her thick, zip-up jacket. 'Luke's always late to every meeting.'

'I'm not shocked at that, but I am surprised at Sasha.' He glared at the phone. 'She's turned her phone off.'

Elfie remembered that she was his PA, and on his payroll. She looked at his irritated frown and sensed that he wasn't used to being messed around.

He glanced at her. 'Well I'm not waiting. We're meeting Doležal at eleven and I want to allow for traffic. Come on.' He set off down the stairs.

Elfie cursed Luke under her breath. Not only was he making the University look bad, she now had to spend even more time with Gabriel on her own!

★ ★ ★

They reached Karlstein Castle with about fifteen minutes to spare. The journey had been relatively uneventful. They had been picked up by the same black car that had collected them from the airport, complete with driver. Gabriel had sat with her in the back this time, but had spent most of the journey making phone calls relating to his business.

He had apologised to her, but she was actually quite happy to avoid talking and look through the magazine she had in her bag, although she did have one ear on his conversations. He sounded very professional, she thought as she flicked through the pages; talking about advertising, marketing, exchange rates and all sorts of things she had only ever heard about on the morning news.

When she first spotted Karlstein Castle out of the window, her eyes widened. Sited high on a hill, the area was dusted with snow and it looked like something out of a fairytale, with sparkling spires and silver crenellations.

'Wow,' she said, impressed, 'you sure know some fancy people.'

'Mm,' he grunted offhandedly.

She frowned at him. 'What happened between you and Doležal?'

'Long story.' Clearly he didn't want to elaborate.

Well that was his prerogative, she

thought; she could hardly blame him for not opening up to her when she was trying to keep the conversation away from personal matters.

The driver pulled up at a barrier and said something to the guard in the box beside the road. The guard nodded and pressed a button, raising the barrier, and the car then wound up the road towards the castle. Passing through a gatehouse, it parked in front of a collection of white stone buildings. Gabriel got out and Elfie followed. It was icy cold, the ground covered in snow, and she was glad she'd worn her boots.

A man was waiting for them and he led them into the buildings. Elfie admired the Gothic architecture as they passed under wide pointed archways, through a maze of rooms and in to a more modern section of the castle. She glanced at Gabriel. He was quiet and his sense of humour seemed to have vanished. When he saw her look at him, however, he smiled, but she could sense his apprehension. There was so much more to this than the Buckle, she thought.

Their guide took them through a group of richly decorated rooms and eventually into an elaborate office, with a huge desk in one corner, fronted by a couple of chairs. The room oozed money from the mahogany furniture to the thick rugs to the expensive paintings on the wall.

'The Count will be with you shortly,' the man told them before withdrawing and leaving them alone.

Gabriel watched him go. Elfie took a seat, but he remained standing. 'He'll make me wait,' he said.

Elfie said nothing. He didn't seem to want to talk. She sat in silence for about five minutes, too nervous to get her magazine out again. She took the time to study Gabriel where he stood by the window, looking at the view, although she was sure he was actually seeing something else in his mind's eye. Clearly he and the Count had a history, and their last meeting had not gone well. Did he really think Doležal was going to sell him the Buckle?

Eventually the door opened, making her jump, and she looked up to see the Count come through, carrying a briefcase in one hand. He was quite tall, almost the same height as Gabriel, and slender, with thick, dark hair that came to a raven's peak on his forehead. He immediately made Elfie think of Dracula. Being called the Count didn't help, she thought, standing as he came into the room.

He walked up to Gabriel and they stood facing each other. Elfie looked from one to the other. Gabriel's face was impassive and she couldn't tell what he was thinking. The Count looked slightly amused, his thin lips curling wryly at the corner. There was something almost medieval about the way the two men were looking at each other. She wouldn't have been at all surprised if one of them had called the other out to a duel.

'Carter,' said Doležal. He held out a hand.

Gabriel hesitated for a moment, then shook it.

Doležal smiled. 'It has been a while,' he said in English, with a heavy Czech accent.

'Not as long as I would have liked,' said Gabriel, not smiling back.

Doležal grinned, then turned to Elfie. His gaze ran up and down her briefly before he held out his hand. 'And you are?'

'This is Dr Summers,' said Gabriel formally. So no first name terms then, Elfie thought. 'From the University of Exeter.'

'Ah, the Anglo-Saxon expert.' Doležal bent over her hand and kissed the air an inch above her fingertips. 'Pleasure,' he said. Elfie fought the urge to snatch her fingers away, certain he was going to turn into a bat any moment.

The Count went behind his desk and sat in the big leather swivel chair, placing the briefcase on the desk. He indicated the seats opposite him and Gabriel and Elfie sat.

'How have you been?' Doležal said.

Gabriel leaned back in his chair and linked his hands. 'I'd rather dispense with the pleasantries, if that's okay?'

Doležal shrugged. 'Of course. A businessman, as always.'

Gabriel stiffened. Elfie frowned. What was insulting about that? Doležal watched him, waiting for his reaction, still amused, swivelling his chair slightly from side to side.

For a while Gabriel said nothing. She got the impression that he was trying to decide whether to react to whatever slight he felt the Count had just given him. Eventually however, he shifted in his chair and she realised he had decided to let it pass. 'Do you have it?' he asked bluntly instead.

Doležal unclicked the briefcase, lifted the lid and looked at the contents, then turned the case around to face them.

Elfie looked at Gabriel. He was staring at the case but didn't seem inclined to move. He glanced up at her. She got out of her chair and walked up to the desk, looking inside.

She held her breath. Lying on the black velvet interior was a magnificent ancient gold belt buckle.

She looked across at Gabriel, who gestured towards the item as if to say, *Go on!* The Count shrugged. 'By all means, examine it.'

Her mouth had gone dry. She reached for her bag and ferreted inside until she found her loupe — a small magnifying glass set in an eyepiece. Her fingers hovered over the Buckle. Suddenly she remembered the myth surrounding its history. She glanced back at Gabriel. For the first time since arriving at the castle, he looked amused and raised an eyebrow at her.

Was she going to let a stupid story stop her from taking this chance to touch an ancient artefact? Elfie gave him an exasperated glare, sighed, then picked the Buckle up. She weighed it in her hands, then brought the loupe up to

Current Transactions

Branch: Maidstone – Kent History & Library Centre

Date: 7/12/2023   Time: 2:00 PM

Name: Bhosale, Manjusha

ID: ...0361

ON LOAN   DUE DATE

Gift of the Nile [text(lar... 28 Dec 2023
C161039640

Bohemian rhapsody [text(la... 28 Dec 2023
C155327215

To renew your items please log onto My Account on the OPAC at
https://kent.spydus.co.uk

www.kent.gov.uk/libraries

Current
Transactions

her eye and examined the intricate detail on the surface.

'What can you tell us about it?' Gabriel asked after a while.

She lowered the loupe, turning the Buckle over in her hands. 'It's heavy; just under half a kilo, I reckon. Twelve to thirteen centimetres long. A tad smaller than the Sutton Hoo one, but not by much. It's gold with ten to fifteen per cent silver — that's what gives it its pale colour. It's hollow, made in two parts joined by a hinge here.' She showed Gabriel the back beneath the loop. 'The pattern is zoomorphic interlace — intertwining snakes and four-legged beasts. The bodies are inlaid with niello — that's a black metallic alloy. The animals are different to the ones on the Sutton Hoo Buckle, though fairly similar. They were probably made by the same artist as part of a pair.' She looked up at him. 'It's genuine. It's not a fake.'

'Of course,' said Doležal impatiently. 'I paid a great deal of money for it.'

Elfie ran her thumb over it. Was it really possible that Charlemagne had brought it here to Prague and had given it to the Princess Libuse? Many myths are actually founded on historical fact, she knew. There was probably more than a grain of truth to it.

Reluctantly, she placed it back on the black velvet and sat down. Her fingers continued to tingle strangely, though.

Doležal leaned forward on the desk. 'So you have seen the Buckle,' he said to Gabriel. 'Now, what else can I do for you?'

'I want to buy it.'

Elfie looked at him in surprise. Clearly this was the first time he had mentioned it to the Count, although she had assumed that the reason they were there was to secure a sale.

Doležal sat back. 'It is not for sale.'

'Everything is for sale at the right price.'

'Not this.'

Gabriel studied him. 'I know how much you paid for it. I will double it.'

Doležal shook his head. 'Not enough.'

'Treble it, then.'

Doležal shook his head again.

Gabriel didn't seem dismayed, as if he had expected the Count to barter, and added, 'Name your price.'

Doležal hesitated, then named a figure so high that Elfie very nearly fell out of her chair.

Gabriel, however, didn't bat an eyelid. 'Okay.'

Doležal stared at him. He pushed himself to his feet and walked around the table, laughing. 'Now you are being ridiculous.'

Gabriel also got to his feet as Doležal approached. 'I am willing to pay.'

'I have already told you, it is not for sale.'

The two men faced each other, about a foot apart. Elfie got up and stood to one side, feeling suddenly nervous.

Gabriel studied the Count with narrowed eyes. 'I want that Buckle.'

'I don't care.'

'You owe me, Doležal.'

The Count glared at him. 'I'm sorry Juliet died, Gabriel, but I'm not selling. And I think it is time for you to go.' His eyes trailed to Elfie. 'Pleased to have met you, Dr Summers.' His eyes ran over her approvingly. 'I don't suppose you are free tonight — would you care to come to dinner?'

Gabriel moved before Elfie had a chance to say anything. He pushed the Count hard in the chest so the other man stumbled back into his desk and before he could recover, Gabriel's fist met his face with a resounding crack.

Elfie squealed, her hands coming up to cover her mouth. Doležal fell backwards, landing in a heap on the floor. Gabriel stood over him, hands clenched, his face finally showing some emotion: pure, unadulterated fury.

Doležal touched his hand to his mouth, wincing as it came away red. He looked across at Elfie, then up at Gabriel and to Elfie's surprise, a self-satisfied smile touched his mouth, as Gabriel hovered over him.

Elfie stepped forwards and touched Gabriel's arm. 'Come on, let's go.'

He looked over at her, met her eyes. As he saw her concern, some of his anger diffused. He looked back down at the Count. 'This isn't over.'

'Get out of my office,' snarled Doležal.

Without another word Gabriel turned and walked out.

Elfie picked up her bag. Backing out, taking one last, longing look at the Buckle, she turned and followed him.

6

Elfie followed Gabriel back to the car. By the thunderous look on his face and the way that he kicked a stone violently out of the way, she guessed that he didn't want to talk about what had just transpired with Doležal.

She slid into the back of the car, quietly getting the magazine out of her bag and pretending to read it while he got in next to her and barked to the driver to get going. He took out his BlackBerry while the car weaved down the long drive and out through the barrier, heading for the city centre.

She tried to read about the recent excavation at the Neolithic settlement of Skara Brae in the Orkneys, but the words kept blurring before her eyes. She glanced across at him. He was busy texting someone, then shortly afterwards he made a phone call about something completely unrelated to what had just happened, barking orders about his business to whoever was on the other end of the phone.

She closed the magazine and looked instead out of the window. She felt hurt and annoyed that he hadn't told her anything about why he had got so angry with the Count. But then, she thought, she was only here on business, wasn't she? Why should he confide in her? Sure, it was rather rude, but in spite of his words on the Charles Bridge, they weren't really friends and had only known each other for a couple of days. She was hardly his confidante.

Still, she felt put in her place and quietly ignored him, aware that the atmosphere inside the car was almost as frosty as the one outside.

Before long they arrived outside the hotel and Elfie immediately jumped out after thanking the driver. She walked up the stairs without waiting for Gabriel and into the hotel, heading straight for the stairs up to the next floor.

Footsteps sounded on the marble steps behind her, and then he appeared at her side, but still he didn't say anything. In silence they got to the top and turned into the corridor.

There, ahead of them, were Sasha and Luke, talking outside her room.

Gabriel stopped abruptly, then walked straight up to them. 'Where the hell were you two?' he demanded.

Luke looked at him, eyebrows raised. 'I came down to the lobby but you'd already gone.'

'I said to meet me there at ten o'clock.'

'Hey dude, I was about ten minutes late, that's hardly a hanging offence.'

Gabriel ignored him and turned to his PA. 'And what's your excuse?'

For once the elegant Sasha looked awkward and ill-at-ease. 'I'm sorry Gabe,' she stuttered, 'I didn't realise how late it was.'

He gave her an icy look. 'Well next time you find the urge to spend the night with a stranger, do it in your own time.'

Sasha stared at him, mouth open, her face scarlet. 'But I wasn't . . . '

He raised an eyebrow at her and her words trailed off. She looked down at the floor, embarrassed and humiliated. He glanced at Luke, who grinned, then Gabriel turned and walked back to his own room, swiped his key card and let himself in.

Elfie walked up and caught the door before it clicked shut. Sasha had turned away, her hand pressed to her mouth, and Luke was now consoling her, leading her back to her own room. Elfie gave a wry smile. Clearly Gabriel had hit the elegantly dressed nail on the head. Trust Luke to move in on Sasha. Although she was surprised that Sasha had acquiesced so quickly. Was she trying to make Gabriel jealous?

Elfie pushed open Gabriel's door and slipped inside. He had ripped off his tie and was now pacing the floor angrily. He looked over in surprise as she let the door click behind her.

He glared at her. 'Come in, why don't you?'

She walked in a little way. 'I'm here to tell you to stop being such an ass!'

He stared at her. 'Excuse me?'

'You heard me. Poor Sasha — you just embarrassed her in public. So she made a mistake — she's only human; she didn't deserve that.'

He turned away and slipped off his jacket, hanging it over a chair. 'I pay her to make my life easier. It's her job, and if she can't do her job, she's not much use to me.'

'That's unfair, and you know it.'

'Do I?' He undid his top button so forcefully the button pinged off across the room, although he didn't seem to notice. 'She gets paid three times what you do — do you still feel the same way now?'

'As I've already told you,' she snapped, 'money means nothing to me. But you think if you pay someone enough they'll do anything, like that Doležal guy back there. He didn't want

104

to sell his stupid Buckle, but you seemed to be convinced that if you kept upping the price, he'd cave in.'

He went very still. 'You know nothing about the situation, sweetheart, so I suggest you stop right there.'

She knew she was taking her life in her hands — his eyes were blazing and he suddenly seemed very tall and powerful. His white shirt made his skin look very brown, and she could see from where the cotton stretched across his chest and arms that he clearly worked out.

He was gorgeous, she thought distractedly; he was the sort of man she had only ever seen on the cover of women's magazines . . . What was she thinking? She shook her head, trying to drag her thoughts back to the conversation. 'Of course I don't. Because you haven't told me anything. I only know what I've seen — that you think you can have anything if you want it enough or pay enough.'

He considered her words. 'Yes, I'd

have to agree with that.' His eyes lingered on her and he smiled greedily.

'Well not me,' she said firmly. 'I'm not for sale.'

'I wouldn't dream of offering you money.' He walked towards her. 'But there's more than one way to skin a rather beautiful cat.'

'What do you mean?' She started to back away. Unfortunately the wall was closer than she thought and she met it with a bump. She watched him advance in alarm. He was still furious, she realised, and now all that fury, all that emotion, was turned on her. Why on earth had she gone into his room?

He stopped about six inches from her. His eyes were so hot they could have melted the ice on the windowsill. He was dangerous, she thought; like an arrow notched and pulled back on the bowstring, ready to be fired.

Did he know how devastatingly attractive he was? He was George Clooney, Brad Pitt and Hugh Jackman rolled into one. Did he know how he made her weak at the knees?

'I mean seduction,' he said huskily.

Elfie felt her cheeks grow scarlet. Oh, dear Lord. She was in trouble now. She was like someone who had never skied before being dumped on the highest slope. She put her hands on his chest to push him away, realising immediately that was a mistake as she felt his firm chest muscles beneath her fingers. 'I would never . . .'

'We'll see,' he said. Catching her wrists with a move so smooth it made her gasp, he pinned her arms behind her back and lowered his lips to hers.

It was nothing like the kiss in the restaurant, when they were dancing. That had been considerate and gentle, slow and luxurious, like swimming in melted chocolate. This was possessive and as she gasped at his sheer audacity her mouth opened under his and he took the opportunity to deepen his kiss. He released her hands and pulled her to him roughly, pressing one hand in the small of her back, pressing her hips to his and leaving her in no doubt how much he desired her!

Elfie pushed against his chest, but he was like a brick wall and she couldn't move him. Her senses were completely overwhelmed. The taste of him and the smell of him was just divine, and made her head spin. The hardness of him as he pressed her against the wall aroused her own passions and she had to fight against a natural instinct to wrap herself around him.

His hand cradling her head caught the scrunchie that was restraining her hair and pulled it out. Releasing her lips, he spread her hair across her shoulders. 'Like fire,' he murmured. He deftly removed her glasses and threw them on the bed.

'Gabriel!' It was the only word her brain could form before he lowered his lips again. As he kissed her, his hand moved from her hair to her neck. Swiftly, he unzipped her jacket. His hand slipped inside, sliding down her ribcage and around her waist. She knew he would be able to feel the thunder of her heart beneath his palm.

He left her lips to kiss her face, her ear, her neck, and she tipped her head back, trying to remember to breathe. It was as if all the air had been sucked from the room. She had to stop him — she would pass out if he carried on!

'Gabriel,' she said again, but he wasn't listening. He kissed back to her lips again, hot with desire.

'Do you want me to stop?' he murmured, kissing her eyelids, her cheeks.

'I . . . ' Suddenly she remembered what he had said. *I mean seduction.* Was he just proving a point — was that all this was?

Putting her hands on his chest, she shoved him as hard as she could. He moved back a little and looked down at her, puzzled.

'Stop it!' she said, her fingers brushing her mouth. Her lips felt bruised and tears came to her eyes.

He frowned and sighed, running a

hand through his hair. 'Elfie . . . '

She bit her lip and walked around him, picking up her glasses and heading for the door.

'Wait, please.'

She stopped, still facing away from him. 'Are you happy now?' she whispered. 'Smug now you've proved your point?' Her blood still surged through her body and she felt an unusual ache in the pit of her stomach.

'I'm sorry.' He walked up behind her, resting light hands on her shoulders. 'I'm in a foul mood and I'm taking it out on you. I apologise. I shouldn't have done that.'

'No, you shouldn't have.' Her arms were wrapped tight around herself and she was trying very hard not to cry.

He turned her very gently until she faced him, then put his arms around her. 'Come here. I'm sorry.'

She leaned her head on his chest and for a moment she felt very confused. Suddenly he was the perfect gentleman again. His lips were resting lightly on her hair and his arms were gentle. She didn't know whether to slap him or kiss him. She pulled away, running her hands over her face, smoothing away her tears.

When she looked up at him, he looked suitably contrite. They studied each other for a moment. She saw the pain in his eyes, and knew that he was still hurting from the meeting with Doležal. 'Why don't you just tell me what happened between you and the Count?' she asked.

He sighed. Walking over to the bed, he sat down, leaning forward, elbows on his knees. 'Doležal and Juliet had an affair,' he said.

Elfie stared at him. Slowly she walked over and sat beside him.

'I'd been to Karlstein a few times, trying to negotiate buying a few artefacts. One day I took Juliet with me. She and Doležal . . . they hit it off, shall we say? I was pleased, idiot that I am; I thought it might help with making a deal. I didn't know that she went back there later and met with him. He told her I paid too much attention to my business and not enough to her. That's why I got annoyed today.'

Elfie sighed. 'Why didn't you tell me?'

'It's not something a man likes to admit,' he said wryly. 'But that's not the worst of it. Juliet fell for him, badly. She was going to leave me. Then she found out she had cancer. When she told Doležal, he didn't want to know. He didn't want to nurse a dying woman and he threw her out.'

'So she came to you,' Elfie said softly.

'Yes.' Gabriel studied his hands.

'And you took her back.'

'She was dying. I'm not a monster.' He cleared his throat.

Elfie thought about how he had reacted when Doležal asked her over for dinner. It must have been the ultimate insult after the Count had already stolen his wife. After all Doležal didn't know the status of their relationship; that they had only just met.

She shivered. 'I wondered why I disliked him so much at first sight. He reminded me of Dracula.'

Gabriel looked at her and gave a small laugh. 'That's possibly the nicest thing anyone's ever said to me.'

She smiled. Taking a deep breath, she reached out and covered his hands with her own. 'I'm sorry. It must have been very difficult for you.'

He took her hand in his own. It looked small and pale next to his large, brown hands. 'It wasn't an easy time.'

Something was still puzzling her. 'So why drag it all up again by going back there? Is it about revenge? He took something of yours so you want to do the same?'

'No. I just really want that Buckle.'

'It was indeed beautiful,' she agreed with a sigh.

'Wasn't it?'

'I still don't agree with private ownership of artefacts,' she warned him. 'But I admit that it was a wonderful piece.'

He studied her, some of his amusement coming back. 'You held it, too.'

She gave him an exasperated look, pulling back her hand. 'Which means absolutely nothing.'

He laughed and she stood, relieved that the black cloud that had been hanging over his head since that morning seemed to have lifted a little.

'Are you going to apologise to Sasha?' she prompted.

He stood. 'Yes, ma'am, in a minute.' He came a bit closer. 'And I'm sorry if I upset you. I seem to be doing a lot of that this weekend.'

'Forget it,' she said with a shrug.

'I didn't kiss you just to prove a point,' he said softly.

Her eyes met his. 'I know,' she whispered. She turned and walked to the door. There she turned and paused. 'What time are we going out tonight?'

'The opera starts at seven. Meet you at six in the lobby?' He smiled at her. 'Are you going to read for a while?'

'No.' She took a deep breath. 'I'm

going shopping.'

He raised an eyebrow, but didn't comment on the fact that clearly shopping wasn't usually on her list of priorities. 'Please, take the car. Tesar will take you anywhere you want.'

'Thank you.' She nodded and slipped outside.

In the corridor, she paused and took the first real deep breath she had taken since walking into his room.

'Ooh,' said someone from further down the corridor. 'Interesting.'

She turned to see Luke walking towards her. He had been heading for the stairs but now came back to see her.

'Looks like we're both being clandestine this weekend,' he said, half-amused, half-put out by seeing her coming out of Gabriel's room, her hair still around her shoulders.

'Not all of us are that easy,' she snapped.

He laughed. 'So you're holding out on him? I'd better wish him luck. Reckon he'll need a blow torch to thaw you out.' His eyes glinted. 'Not that I'd want an ice maiden.'

'Well at least you've got Sasha to warm you,' she said, adding, 'You do know she's in love with Gabriel, right?'

He shrugged. 'What do I care? I'm not going to ask her to marry me.'

'Wow, you're such a charmer, Luke.'

He raised an eyebrow. 'Hey she knew exactly what she was getting into.' He leaned forward as if he was being conspiratorial. 'Just for your info, some women — real women, that is — actually enjoy getting physical without a marriage proposal first.'

Real women? The throwaway comment stung. Luke saw he had hit home and his lip curled. 'Have a great afternoon.' He walked off, whistling.

Elfie let herself into her room and sat on the bed. Her head was buzzing. She thought about Doležal and his affair with Juliet; about Gabriel, promising to seduce her; about Luke, using women as he pleased, sneering at her because she wasn't a 'real woman'; about her

116

father, secretly having an affair with someone else, too cowardly to tell her mother about it.

What was it with men? Elfie had prided herself on the fact that she had managed to remain out of the clutch of love for so long, but suddenly she found herself irritated by Luke's assumptions. It wasn't that she couldn't get a man; it was that she didn't want one.

Gabriel had seen through her attempt at disguise, but she knew that even he — in spite of his protestations — thought her a challenge. Both men saw her as a prim little maid, an experiment for them to test their hypothesis on, until their lust was satisfied. If she gave in to them, what would happen to her; would she be cast off as her mother had been, as Juliet had been?

Standing again, she walked in front of the long mirror behind the door. She studied her reflection thoughtfully. Her image had taken careful cultivation, but suddenly she was tired of being the mousy university professor, interested in nothing but books. She wanted to show everyone that she took that image out of choice — it wasn't forced upon her.

She ran a hand through her hair, smoothed down her jumper and trousers. She didn't have a bad figure. If she wanted, she could wear tight clothes and high heels. She could show them what she could really look like, if she tried. Did she have the courage?

Elfie picked up her bag. Smiling, she headed for the door.

7

Elfie headed downstairs to the foyer. Should she take Gabriel up on his offer of the car? It seemed silly not to — God knew where she would end up if she tried going out on her own. She asked at the desk if Tesar was available and he came out immediately, smart in his dark suit and cap, giving her a nice smile.

She knew he spoke English because she had heard Gabriel talking to him. 'I wanted to go shopping,' she said shyly, 'and Mr Carter said you might be able to take me?'

'Of course,' he said, his English impeccable in spite of a strong accent, and he indicated for her to precede him out of the doors. She went out, exclaiming as the cold immediately bit into her face and hands.

Tesar held the car door open for her

and she got in the front seat, feeling odd being a passenger on the right-hand side of the car. He went round and got in the driver's side. Quickly checking his mobile phone, he started the car. 'Now, Dr Summers, where would you like to go?'

'Oh, please, call me Elfie.' But then she hesitated. 'And I'd like to see some fashion boutiques, please — I need something to wear to the opera.'

He studied her, and started to smile. 'Yes, ma'am. I know exactly what you are looking for.' Sliding the car into gear, he headed for the city centre.

Elfie felt nerves begin to build in her stomach. She had never been into a posh boutique in her life. She had always been intimidated by the sort of women who work in those shops, and she even found department stores scary. Her clothes either came from catalogues or second-hand shops — not that she didn't have any money — she had savings — but because clothes had never been important to her.

Tesar drove confidently through the busy Prague streets. She looked across at him. 'Do you work for Gabriel or for the hotel?'

'For Mr Carter, ma'am. I work at his Czech office and I drive him when he is in the city.'

'Have you known him long?' she asked.

'About five years, ma'am.'

'So you . . . knew his wife? Was she very pretty?'

Tesar looked across at her. 'Yes, she was very beautiful.' Of course she was. Elfie nodded, looking out of the window. Tesar cleared his throat, glancing at her. 'She was beautiful here,' he indicated his face. 'But not here.' He touched his chest, over his heart. 'She made him very unhappy.' He looked back at the road, and Elfie got the impression that he suddenly thought he had said too much.

'Thank you,' she said softly, then studying the road ahead, she changed the subject. 'Where are you taking me?'

'My wife's friend works in a small shop called Tatiana's. They will be able to help you find what you need.'

She nodded. Thank goodness she had her Visa card with her!

Within ten minutes Tesar was pulling up a few doors down from the shop. Elfie got out, thinking how beautiful the city was, even in the shopping area. The high buildings had exquisite Baroque architecture, and even the pavement was tiled with elegant grey and cream patterns.

Tesar ushered Elfie over to the shop and went inside, Elfie following him rather nervously.

The interior was small but bright, decorated in white with tasteful pictures of models in the owner's designs on the walls. The two assistants came over as they entered, the younger one coming up to Tesar and kissing him on the cheek. 'Tesar!' she said, following it with a sentence in Czech.

He indicated for Elfie to come forward. 'This is a friend,' he said in

English. 'She is visiting the city and is going to the opera tonight.' He switched to Czech and said a few sentences. Elfie caught the name Gabriel and blushed. The two women looked at her with openly amused interest.

The woman he had kissed held out her hand. 'I am Lida,' she said in English. 'I am sure we can find something here that you will like.'

'Thank you very much,' Elfie said nervously. 'I will need a lot of help, I'm afraid, to be made presentable.'

'Not so much, I think,' said the other, slightly older woman, smiling. 'I am Kalina.' She pushed Tesar towards a chair in the corner. 'You sit there. You can give us your opinion when she is ready!'

Tesar sat and opened a newspaper. Elfie looked at him, worried. 'Won't Mr Carter need you at all? I don't want to take up your time if he's busy.'

In answer he removed his phone, brought up a text and handed it to her. It said simply: *Take all the time she needs*.

She handed him back the phone, feeling herself grow hot. How come Gabriel was able to make her blush from across the other side of the city?

The two women started asking her questions about the sort of things she liked to wear, and what she was looking for. 'I don't know,' Elfie said eventually, embarrassed. 'I don't know what sort of thing to wear. I really don't know anything at all about fashion.'

'It is no matter,' Kalina dismissed. 'We do, so you will be okay, yes?'

She eyed Elfie up and down and went to the rack and began to lift dresses off. 'Come, my dear, let's get you out of that coat and into something a little more elegant.'

For the next hour Elfie thought she must have tried on fifty or so combinations of outfits. She tried trousers and tops, skirts and dresses, with heels, with flats, jackets on and off. Some of the clothing was so unusual that she knew there was no way she could go out in it. Equally some of the colours made her feel too conspicuous, and she knew she wouldn't be comfortable in the deep red dress they made her try on.

'I'd like black,' she said.

Lida waved her hand. 'You want to stand out, no?'

'No,' Elfie said nervously, and they both laughed.

'Of course you do! You want to make the men desire you!'

Elfie blushed again. She had told them briefly about why she wanted to look so different. 'Yes, but I also want to feel comfortable.'

Kalina snapped her fingers. 'I have just the thing!' She scurried out of the dressing room and back into the shop, returning with a dress held aloft. 'What do you think?'

Elfie stared at it. 'It's beautiful,' she admitted. 'But . . . '

'Quick, try it on!'

She let them slip it over her head and then stood in front of the mirror. It was a dark emerald green, exactly the same colour as her eyes. It was strapless and consisted of several layers of chiffon that floated around her figure, ending just below the knee.

'Heels,' said Lida, running into the shop and returning with a pair of strappy sandals with an enclosed toe. 'You can wear pantyhose with these, after all, it is cold.'

Elfie slipped them on. She didn't wear heels very often; luckily they weren't too high, but they did make her feel more feminine. Kalina spread her hair around her shoulders. 'Come with me.' She led her into the shop.

Tesar glanced up from his paper, starting to get bored after so many outfits, but as he caught sight of her, he stared, his paper sinking to his lap.

'Yes,' said Lida and Kalina together, laughing.

Elfie let them find her a sumptuous wrap for her as well and, as she paid in a daze, wondering if her Visa would go into meltdown, Kalina said, 'Now I have a suggestion to make — there is a hair salon just down the road. Why don't you go and get your hair cut properly? You can collect this outfit on the way back.'

Elfie touched her red locks self consciously. 'I don't want it short.'

'I don't mean short. Just neat,' Kalina said. 'It will be the finishing touch.'

★　★　★

At ten-to-six, Elfie stood in front of the mirror. She had put on the new underwear that Kalina had suggested — a cream strapless bra, sheer, almost pointless lacy knickers and sheer tights — and then slipped on the green dress, letting the chiffon layers float around her in waves. She slid her feet into the new shoes, then looked at her reflection.

The stylist had left her hair long, but trimmed and layered it gently so that she had soft wisps framing her face. It was an improvement, she had to admit. She barely recognised herself.

They had also had a make-up

specialist there, who had shown her some basic techniques in applying liner and mascara subtly, as she was so unused to wearing it, and she had also been told firmly not to wear her glasses. She turned from side to side — then suddenly sank onto the bed, her face in her hands.

What on earth was she doing? Part of her wanted to rip everything off. She felt ashamed of herself. This wasn't her; Dr Summers didn't do things like this. She wore baggy tops and trousers and glasses. What was she trying to prove?

But another part of her was thrilled to see herself looking so different. She remembered the look on Tesar's face in the shop. She wanted to see that look on Luke's face — and on Gabriel's, more than anything.

Besides, what did it matter what she did? She was in a foreign city, due to fly back on Monday, and she would probably never see Gabriel again. So what if she dressed up for one night? It would be worth it to know that Luke was thinking of her like this every time she walked into his office. At least it would show him that she chose to look the way she did deliberately.

Picking up her new black evening bag, she placed her black wrap around her shoulders and left her room.

She walked down the corridor and started to descend the stairs. It was just six o'clock. As the foyer became visible, she saw immediately that they were all there, waiting for her. Luke and Sasha had their backs to her, Gabriel was sideways on. Sasha was wearing a long scarlet gown that showed her dark complexion off. Judging by the way she was laughing at something Gabriel was saying, Elfie guessed that they had made up.

Though handsome, Luke looked uncomfortable in his dark dress suit, like a beach surfer suddenly forced to meet the Queen. As Elfie watched, he fingered his collar awkwardly. He already looked bored.

Her eyes flicked over to Gabriel. He

was wearing a smart black suit with satin lapels, and a white shirt with a wing-tip collar and black bow tie. His dark hair was brushed up at the front, fashionably ruffled at the back. He looked like a film star, she thought, her heart pounding against her ribs.

At that moment he glanced up at the stairs and caught sight of her. He stopped talking and stared, his eyebrows rising, eyes widening.

Got him, she thought with pleasure.

The other two, realising something had caught his attention, turned and followed his gaze.

Elfie, her heart now trying to leap out of her chest, descended the stairs as gracefully as she could, praying to every God there was that she didn't trip and land flat on her backside.

As she walked up to them, Luke wolf whistled, loudly.

'A bit crude,' said Gabriel, 'but I have to agree with the sentiment.' He smiled at her. 'Had a good afternoon?'

'Very pleasant thank you,' she replied.

He held his arm out to her. His eyes were warm with admiration and amusement. 'Shall we?'

She took his proferred arm, smiling at the other two. Sasha glared at her. Luke seemed too shocked to do anything other than stare.

They went outside into the icy cold air. 'It's definitely going to snow tonight,' Gabriel said, his breath frosting before him. He glanced at her. 'Are you going to be warm enough?'

'I have my own central heating furnace as I'm sure you've spotted by now,' she said wryly, knowing she was blushing.

He laughed, opening the front car door for her. She slid in as elegantly as she could. Gabriel got in the driver's seat.

'No Tesar this evening?'

'I think he was exhausted with all the shopping today,' Gabriel said wryly, starting the engine as the others got in the back. He clipped his seatbelt in, then looked over at her. 'You look

131

wonderful, by the way.'

'Thank you.' She was so glad that she hadn't changed. It had been worth it to see that look on his face when she came down the stairs!

* * *

Elfie loved the opera, enjoying the performance of The Barber of Seville in such a grand setting, even though Luke yawned all the way through it. Afterwards they went to dinner at a small but exclusive restaurant. She had a lovely evening, in spite of the fact that two of the people she was dining with weren't companions she would have chosen.

The conversation remained light and Luke could be funny when he wasn't being an ass, and after a while even Sasha began to relax.

Elfie had thought she would feel awkward in her new outfit, as if people would be pointing at her asking why on earth she was dressed up in such a fancy manner. But of course they didn't, and for the first time in her life she attracted stares as she walked down the road.

It was the dress, of course, she knew; it seemed to have a mind of its own. It wouldn't let her sit in the background like she usually did, content to listen to the conversation around her. The dress wanted to talk, and so for the first time in ages she found herself offering opinions, answering Luke's occasional digs with quips of her own, giving as good as she got.

It was a fascinating thing, to suddenly have this power that she had never known she possessed. When Luke spoke to her, she found that if she leaned forward slightly and looked up at him through her lashes, his acerbic manner vanished and he became almost eager to please, looking to her for approval when he made a joke, brushing her hand occasionally as he reached for his glass. It was an authority she had never thought to have, and it gave her a surge of cruel pleasure to think that for once she was controlling his emotions rather than the other way around.

Towards the end of the dinner she laughed at something he said and then glanced across at Gabriel. He was sitting back in his seat, twirling his low-alcohol beer bottle in one hand, the other arm hooked over the back of his chair, studying her. He had grown progressively quieter through the evening and she realised he had hardly said anything for the past ten minutes.

'Are you okay?'

He didn't answer and gestured at the empty plates and glasses. 'Has everyone finished?' When everyone indicated that they had, he stood and they all followed.

Elfie felt suddenly uneasy. Had she upset him in some way?

As he paid, Luke took the car keys and escorted Sasha out of the restaurant to the car. Elfie hovered, wondering whether to wait for Gabriel, hesitant as she saw him glance over at her. His mood had darkened, she could easily tell.

When he had finished, he came over to her and took her arm, directing her towards the door.

'What's the matter?' she said impatiently, trying to remove her arm from his tight grip.

'Are you enjoying yourself?'

She frowned. 'Yes thank you, I've had a lovely evening — up until now.'

Outside the restaurant, he turned her suddenly and pushed her in the corner of the wall, out of sight of the car. 'What are you doing?' he snapped.

'What?'

'Don't pretend you don't know. Flirting with Luke, batting your eyelashes at him,' he snarled.

'So what if I am?' she said hotly, lifting her chin.

'Is that what you wanted?' he said huskily, stepping closer to her, pinning her in the corner. 'To have all the men in the restaurant staring at you, including me; to have Luke hanging on your every word?'

She met his eyes, dark as melted chocolate. 'Yes.'

His eyes rested on her lips. 'Well it worked.'

'I know.'

His eyes narrowed. 'It's a dangerous game you're playing. I hope you know what you're doing.'

She suddenly, desperately, wanted him to kiss her. But he wasn't going to, she realised. He was angry with her for flirting with Luke. He was going to simply walk away.

Before she could think better of it, she leaned forward and touched her lips to his. With her heels on she was only a couple of inches shorter than him and she only had to stretch up a little.

This time it was his turn to breathe in sharply. She wondered if he would pull back or push her away, but he didn't. Neither did he gather her in his arms. He just stood there and let her kiss him.

When she stepped back, he studied

her thoughtfully.

'It's the dress,' she apologised. 'Sorry. It has a mind of its own.'

'Perhaps you should wear it more often.' He gave her a wry smile. 'Come on, the other two will be waiting.'

They drove back in silence. Sasha was almost asleep, curled up against Luke. Gabriel studied the road and didn't seem inclined to talk. Elfie studied the beautiful architecture but her thoughts kept slipping back to how his lips had felt against hers.

Back at the hotel, they made their way upstairs. Luke opened Sasha's room for her and disappeared inside after wishing them goodnight. Gabriel watched them go, then glanced back at Elfie. He looked at his watch. 'I'd ask you for a drink downstairs, but I'm afraid there's something I've got to do,' he said. He swiped his keycard and opened his door. 'Thank you for a lovely evening.'

She felt a wave of disappointment. Was the evening coming to an end? It was only eleven o'clock. 'Okay. Do you have a meeting or something?'

He smiled wryly. 'Kind of. I have something to collect, and I'm on a tight schedule, sorry. If you're still up when I get back, I'll be in the bar.'

He disappeared inside his room. Once again she caught the door before it closed and slipped inside.

'You're going to Karlstein,' she said.

He turned and gave her an exasperated look. 'Once again, come in, why don't you?' He slipped off his jacket and began to undo his bow tie.

'Well, aren't you?'

He glanced over at her. 'So what if I am?' He echoed her earlier words.

'You're going to steal the Buckle?' she gasped.

'I'm not a thief,' he said wryly. He started to unbutton his shirt. Then he grinned. 'I'll leave a cheque in its place.'

She stared at him as a peculiar pool of excitement stirred in her stomach. 'You're crazy,' she said.

He shrugged. 'The bastard owes me.'

He slipped his shirt off his shoulders and threw it on the bed.

She studied his well defined muscles. 'How are you going to get in?'

'Someone's going to leave a few doors open for me.'

'You bought one of the guards?' He shrugged, but his smile told her she was right. She watched him go over to the chest of drawers and take out a black jumper. 'I'm coming with you,' she said as he pulled it over his head.

He laughed, ruffling his hair back into place. 'No, you're not.'

'Yes I am. I want to make sure he hasn't switched it with a fake one.'

He paused and looked at her. She met his gaze evenly. A smile gradually grew on his face. He looked at her dress. 'Well you can't go like that.'

'Fair enough. Give me two minutes.'

8

Elfie hurriedly let herself into her own room. She dropped the wrap and reluctantly lifted her dress off, letting it fall onto the bed, then slipped off her tights. What did she have to wear that was black? She rifled through her suitcase. She had black leggings which she had brought to wear beneath her trousers if it was really cold. She pulled those on, then extracted the black roll-neck jumper that she usually wore under a multi-coloured oversize sweater and pulled it on. She tugged on thick socks and her black boots and looked at herself in the mirror. The outfit was exceedingly clinging, but at least it was all black.

Scooping her hair back into her usual scrunchie, she grabbed her bag and the wrap and left her room again. Gabriel was already in the corridor. He had changed into black jeans and his big black coat, and was examining the contents of a briefcase, which he now snapped shut as he saw her emerge.

He stared at her as she let the door close behind her. She looked down at her outfit. 'What? Sorry, it's all I had in black.'

He closed his eyes for a moment, inhaling. As he exhaled he opened them, meeting her gaze with his hot, chocolate stare. 'You were sent here to torture me,' he replied, holding out a hand. She slid hers into his shyly. 'Come on,' he said, smiling, 'let's get this over with.'

★　★　★

Karlstein Castle was in semi-darkness as they drove up to it. She checked her watch and saw it was almost midnight. As he pulled up to the barrier, it raised immediately, the guard clearly expecting him. He grinned at her and continued up to the place where they had parked earlier that day.

They got out. It had been snowing harder there, and her boots crunched on it's hard white surface. He grabbed her hand and led her over to a door in the side of a wall. He checked his watch. Then, quietly, he tapped three times on the wood. The door immediately opened and he slipped inside, pulling her with him. Elfie recognised the man who had shown them into Doležal's office that morning.

'Mr Carter,' the man whispered. He gave Gabriel a card like a credit card.

Gabriel nodded his thanks. He gave the man a brown paper envelope. The man went through the door, disappearing down the hill. Gabriel turned to Elfie. 'We're on our own now.'

She followed him into the building. He walked softly along the corridor and turned left, through another door and then she recognised the area that they had entered that morning.

'Won't he have locked the Buckle away with his main collection?' she whispered anxiously.

'No. That's on the other side of the castle. He keeps his latest pieces — the ones he hasn't got round to displaying yet — in a room by his private apartment.' He paused by a door, listened for a moment, then opened it.

They made their way through a series of rooms, Elfie beginning to wonder how on earth he remembered where to go, and hoping that he didn't leave her there because there was no way she'd find her own way out.

He used the card the man had given him twice; once to pass through a door leading to the inner sanctum, and again when they obviously reached Doležal's private apartments.

'Is he here at the castle?' she whispered as they crept carefully into the study they had entered that morning.

'Probably.'

She followed Gabriel nervously. 'Do you do this sort of thing often?'

He flashed her an amused grin. 'First time, actually.' He laughed softly, then pushed open the door that Doležal had entered through that morning. They were in a smaller study. On the opposite door was a box with a combination keypad. Gabriel walked across this room, set his briefcase on the floor and opened it, retrieving a contraption that he fixed to the pad.

Elfie watched, amazed, as he linked in a couple of wires, then pressed a button, starting the combination decoder.

'Very James Bond,' she said, impressed.

He winked. The decoder gradually worked through the numbers, then there was a click, and the door unlocked audibly. He opened it, turning on the light. He peered round, then turned and beckoned her in.

It was a large storage room, a table in the centre, the walls lined with shelves filled with black boxes. They were all numbered.

'What number is the Buckle in?'

'Eighty two,' he said. Together they began searching the shelves.

'Got it,' he said after a minute or so.

He slid the box out and laid it on the table. Once again he opened his own briefcase, retrieving a set of keys. He selected one, then slid it into the lock on the black box.

It clicked open.

His eyes met hers as he raised the lid. She glanced down, holding her breath. There lay the Buckle, glittering in the electric light.

She lifted it up gently, turning it over in her hands, examining the intricate design, felt the weight and looked at the hinge. 'It's real.' She held it out to him and he took it.

He sighed. 'It's beautiful.' He took something out of his pocket and put it where the Buckle had been resting. It was a cheque, she saw, for a shocking amount of money.

'You realise you're holding it now,' she whispered to him.

He raised his gaze, meeting hers. His warm, chocolate brown eyes showed his amusement. 'So I am.' He opened his mouth to say something else, but at that moment they heard a sound from an adjoining room.

They both froze. Gabriel moved soundlessly to the wall and turned out the light. Leaving his briefcase behind, he tucked the Buckle into his jeans pocket. He reached out and took her hand, then cautiously slipped through the door. They were just crossing the room when a door that they hadn't seen on the other side of the room opened.

'Run!'

Gabriel pushed her in front of him. Panic rising within her, she started running back the way they had come. She clearly heard Doležal's angry shout. 'Which way?' she cried. Gabriel started to lead, pulling her with him as he threaded his way through the maze of rooms. They managed to get all the way to the outside wall before Doležal reached them.

Gabriel flung open the outer door. Elfie turned to see how far behind them the Count was and squealed as she saw him hot on their heels. But that wasn't the worst part of it — he was carrying a gun!

'Gabriel!'

'I know.' He pushed her in front of him again as they ran across the open yard towards the car.

The gun fired. A bullet thudded into the wall nearby — a warning shot, she realised. Gabriel turned, pushing her behind him. He held up his hands.

Doležal walked towards them, the gun pointing at Gabriel. His face was thunderous. 'Give me back the Buckle!'

'No.'

Doležal stood two feet in front of him. 'Give me back the Buckle, or I will shoot you right here, right now. Do you want to die over the damn thing?'

Gabriel was breathing heavily, but when he spoke his voice was calm. 'No, and I'm sure you don't want to kill me over it.'

'Would you care to bet?'

Elfie leaned her forehead against Gabriel's back in shock; this was so not a game anymore.

He looked over his shoulder at her. 'Get in the car.'

'Gabriel . . . '

'Elfie, get in the car.'

She did so, sliding in hurriedly, turning in the seat to watch them.

Gabriel studied his old enemy thoughtfully. 'I'm going to walk around the other side of the car now,' he said.

'Stay where you are!'

Gabriel started moving around the boot towards the driver's side.

Doležal walked with him, gesturing angrily with the gun. 'Don't move!'

'I'm going to get my keys out of my pocket.'

'Don't move!' yelled Doležal.

Gabriel lowered his hand carefully and pulled the keys out, then slowly opened the car door.

The Count was physically shaking. 'I will shoot you.'

Gabriel paused. 'No you won't. Because you owe me one, Václav. Juliet died saying your name, did you know that?' Doležal said nothing, his finger twitching on the trigger. 'Did you know that she was pregnant with your child when she was diagnosed?' Gabriel said softly.

Elfie gasped, her hand flying up to cover her mouth.

Doležal stared at him. 'You're lying.'

'It's the truth. She didn't tell you because she didn't want to trap you into looking after her. She had to abort it, because of the treatment. She didn't want you to know.' His voice was very hard. 'But I thought that you should.'

Doležal didn't move. Then, slowly, he lowered his arm.

The two men stared at each other. Gabriel turned and got into the car. Starting the engine, he reversed back and then screeched off down the long drive. In the wing mirror Elfie saw Doležal still standing watching them until they disappeared.

Elfie finally let out the long breath that she had been holding. She looked across at him. He glanced at her, giving a wry laugh.

'I thought we were dead meat,' she said, still shaking. She studied him as he slowed at the barrier, watching it rise, then speeding up the car again. 'Was that the truth? Was Juliet really pregnant by him or did you just make it up to get away?'

He changed gear and sighed. 'It was the truth.'

'How did she know it was his?'

'Because we hadn't slept together for over six months.'

'Oh.'

He glanced at her again and smiled, reaching out a hand to hold hers. 'Water under the bridge,' he said. 'It's done now.'

'So he won't come after you, for the Buckle? You don't think he'll call the police or anything?'

'No. Guilt does strange things to a man.' He frowned, but didn't add anything else.

She leaned back in her seat. What an evening! How strange it would be to go back to her tiny flat and her quiet life after this.

It was snowing harder now, and Gabriel drove carefully back into town. 'Do you want to go to the hotel?' he asked out of the blue. 'Or would you like to walk along the river?'

'At midnight? In the snow?'

He shrugged, smiling.

She laughed. 'Okay.'

He parked the car near the hotel but led her away, down the deserted streets towards the bridge. He held her hand as they walked, trying to warm her fingers. 'You should have brought gloves.'

'I didn't know a midnight walk in the freezing cold was in the offing.'

He gave her a regretful look. 'I'm sorry I put you in danger tonight.'

She sighed. 'I insisted on coming, remember? It's my fault.'

'Even so . . . '

She nodded and they continued on in silence. The snow fell softly around them, lining the streets with white.

Turning and going through the Tower, they emerged onto the bridge.

They walked along a little way, then stopped and looked over at the water. It was black and looked icy. She shivered.

'Are you cold?' In spite of her protests, he slipped off his coat and placed it around her shoulders.

'You'll freeze.'

'Ah, but I deserve it.' He pulled the coat close around her.

She glanced around the bridge. 'It's a shame all the stalls have gone. And that man singing love songs. It would have been nice on a night like this.'

'I'll sing to you instead,' he said. He caught her right hand in his left and put his other on her waist beneath the coat.

She laughed. 'You really are crazy.'

'It's the city,' he said. 'Nothing to do with me.' He started to sing Nat King Cole's When I Fall In Love, moving with her in time. She gave in and moved closer, letting him slip his arm around her back. He had a lovely voice. The snow fell softly around them, laying on her shoulders and hair. He must be freezing, she thought, but he wasn't shivering.

Elfie closed her eyes. She wanted the night to go on forever.

As he came to the end of the song, he twirled her gently, bringing her towards him for the final notes. She laughed. 'Nicely done,' she said.

'I thought so.' He studied her for a moment. 'We're on the Charles Bridge, we're criminal masterminds, we've nearly been shot and it's snowing. I can't possibly not kiss you, you know.'

'You needed an excuse?'

His lips curled. 'Not really.'

He pulled her towards him. Slowly he lowered his lips to hers. They were cold. She let her own cold hand come up to rest on his face, feeling the slight stubble there. It was snowing heavily now, a thick layer already forming on his hair.

After a moment, she pulled back from him, smiling. 'Do you have a priceless artefact in your pocket, or are you just pleased to see me?'

He started laughing and pulled out

the Buckle, tilting it so that it caught the light from the lamppost. He caught her hand again. 'Come on, let's get back to the hotel. I need a whisky.'

★ ★ ★

At the hotel, they went into the bar lounge and sat in front of a roaring log fire while he drank whisky and she sipped at a Slivovice, the Buckle lying between them on the seat. It was so lovely and warm there that they stayed, talking, for over an hour, discussing everything from music to books to their favourite historical sites.

Elfie felt herself gradually thawing, and not just physically. The final frozen part of her that she had kept inside for so long had melted at last. Her fingers lingered on the Buckle. She didn't know if she believed that it was the piece of metal that was responsible for her falling in love, but fall in love she had, and she knew there was no going back.

Was this what he had felt for Juliet? Or Juliet for Doležal? Or her father for her mother, or that other woman? Elfie didn't know, and it didn't matter. She and Gabriel were the only thing that was important at that moment.

He was watching her as these thoughts passed through her head, and now he smiled. 'What are you thinking about?'

'Charlemagne,' she said. 'And Libuse.'

He looked down at the Buckle. 'Yes. I wonder if it was true.'

Did he move first or did she? Elfie wasn't sure, but their lips touched, and she tasted the heat of his whisky as he kissed her slowly, luxuriously. It was a kiss that she wanted to go on forever. Well that was impossible, she thought. But it could go on for a few more hours — if she let it.

After a few moments she pulled back. Her heart was thumping. She couldn't believe she was about to say what she was going to say. Was it the brandy's influence, or the Buckle's? Or just the passion in his eyes that warmed her to the core? But she suddenly, desperately, wanted him to do more than kiss her.

She swallowed. 'Shall we go to bed?' He raised an eyebrow. 'I mean, together,' she added helpfully.

He smiled, but his eyes were serious. 'Are you sure?'

She blushed. 'Am I being too forward? Are you shocked?'

He laughed. 'Sweetheart, you're a grown up. There's no right or wrong between two consenting adults. Your life's your own — you don't have to make excuses or justify yourself to me.'

His words warmed her more than the Slivovice. He got up and pulled her with him, tucking the Buckle back in his pocket. Taking her hand, he led her out of the bar and up the stairs.

As they entered the corridor to their rooms, however, her heart sank. Luke was sitting outside her room on the floor, a beer bottle in his hand.

As they walked up, he pushed himself unsteadily to his feet. 'Where the hell have you been?'

Elfie stared at him. 'What's it to you?'

He glared at Gabriel, who raised an eyebrow, then turned his attention back to Elfie. 'I thought . . . after this evening . . . ' He looked back at Gabriel and gave a sharp laugh. 'My mistake. Maybe after you're done with her, mate, you'll pass her on?'

Gabriel stiffened but Elfie was quicker. It was the first time she had slapped a man's face, and the satisfaction was greater than she had expected. Luke's head snapped to one side and the imprint of her fingers reddened on his skin.

'How dare you!' she hissed, furious. 'I've never shown you the slightest bit of interest.'

'You were flirting with me tonight,' he spat at her. 'Leading me on, good and proper. Which is about all you're good at.' He sneered at Gabriel. 'Good luck with her, mate. You'll need a bonfire to melt that ice queen.' He stomped off to his room.

'Luke?'

The Australian turned as Gabriel called his name. 'What?'

'As you missed the meeting this morning, I'm afraid I can't put your stay at the hotel down to expenses. I'll expect you to settle your own bill in the morning.' He casually swiped his card key and backed into his room, pulling Elfie with him. She had one last glimpse of Luke's face, showing astonishment and shock, before the door closed.

9

Closing the door behind them, the two of them burst out laughing. 'That will cost him,' said Gabriel grimly. 'I would think he's made it through a good portion of the minibar by now.'

'You're truly wicked,' she said, her heart beginning to pound again now that they were alone.

He fixed her with his gaze, widening his eyes. 'Do you want to find out just how wicked I can be?'

He slipped his coat that he had wrapped her in earlier off her shoulders. 'You're sure?' he whispered hoarsely, tossing the coat aside and brushing his lips against her hair.

Her heart was beating so loudly she was surprised it hadn't leaped out of her chest and run down the hall. 'A hundred percent,' she said breathlessly.

He grinned and swiftly swept her

jumper over her head, and threw it to the ground. His eyes grew hot as he studied her and she was suddenly very glad that she'd bought new underwear. He ran a light finger over the swell of her breast, making her shiver.

Awkwardly, she pressed herself close to him, pulling up his jumper, desperate to feel his skin against her. He seized the back of the neck and yanked it over his head, throwing it to the ground on top of hers.

She rested her hands on the bare skin of his chest, leaning into him as he wrapped her in his arms. He found the catch on the back of her bra and in one swift movement he pinched it together and it pinged open.

She jumped back with a gasp and brought her hands up to clasp the item to her. 'Clearly you've had some practice!' she said.

'Any man worth his salt can do that,' he scoffed. He pulled her to him, keeping his eyes locked on hers, and pulled the scrunchie out of her hair watching as her flaming locks tumbled around her shoulders. Then he firmly took the bra from her hands and dropped it on top of the rapidly growing pile of clothes on the floor.

He lowered his lips to hers again, his hands warm on her waist. Slowly, she raised her arms around his neck, pressing herself against him. She was rewarded with a long sigh, and he skimmed his hands up her ribcage to cup her breasts. Elfie held her breath but didn't move away, welcoming the hardness of him against her, desire blossoming in her stomach.

He levered off one shoe, then the other, then started to move her backwards until she felt the bed at the back of her legs. Her fingers found the top button of his jeans and she started to try and undo it.

'Let me,' he said and he unzipped his jeans and kicked them off. Naked, he suddenly swept her up into his arms, making her squeal, and lowered her carefully onto the bed, where he lay beside her. 'You still sure?' he asked.

She nodded. 'I'm . . . a bit nervous,' she whispered. 'But . . . I want to.'

He moved closer, his mouth brushing her cheek. 'We'll go slow. I want to make the most of it, anyway.'

He kissed her unhurriedly, lazily, his warm fingers caressing her skin, making her give little gasps. His lips left her mouth to plant small kisses across her cheek and down her neck. He kissed around her breasts, and she looked up at the ceiling, holding her breath and clasping his head with her hands, her fingers tangled in his hair.

Oh, dear Lord, she felt as if she were swimming in melted chocolate. Even in her wildest daydreams, she never thought it could be like this. Why on earth had she waited so long for this? She looked up at him as he began to move, feeling her heart swell at the tender look in his eyes, the passion he was trying so hard to contain so that he didn't hurt her. But it didn't hurt at all, for he was too gentle, and she was too ready for him.

He made love to her tenderly, gradually growing more passionate as his need overwhelmed his attempt at being gentle. Elfie found herself swept up in his desire feeling the tightness building inside her, she let the wave carry her away, holding Gabriel tightly, thinking she had never seen anything as beautiful as him at that moment, dizzy with the knowledge that it was she who had brought him to that peak, running her hands over the tightening muscles in his back.

Afterwards he curled around her, nuzzling her neck, whispering into her hair in the semi darkness as, outside, the snow fell gently, and she drifted slowly to sleep.

★　★　★

When she awoke, it was light. The first thing she saw on her pillow was the Buckle, gleaming gently in the early morning sunshine. She smiled, reached out and took it, then rolled over.

The other side of the bed was empty.

Elfie sat up, holding the quilt to her with the Buckle, looking around the room. Clearly he wasn't in the bathroom as the door was open. She glanced at the floor and saw that it was clear of clothes; her own had been folded and placed on the chair, but his jeans and shoes were gone.

Frowning and getting out of bed, she opened the wardrobe door. The rest of his clothes were still in there, including his coat. At least he hadn't cut and run, she thought bitterly. So where had he gone? Maybe he'd just popped out for something.

She went over to the chair and pulled on her knickers and leggings. At that moment there was a knock at the door.

She froze. It couldn't be him, surely; he would have taken his keycard. Quickly she put on her bra and pulled her black jumper over her head. Then she went to the door and opened it cautiously, peering out.

It was Sasha.

Gabriel's PA smiled at her. She was carrying a tray of breakfast items. Walking past Elfie, she put the tray on the table. 'Good morning!'

Elfie stared at her, lost for words, though Sasha didn't seem to notice. 'There's cooked breakfast and continental,' she said. 'He wasn't sure what you would want.'

Elfie folded her arms across herself protectively. 'Where is he?' she asked softly.

'Oh, he had to go to work. He didn't want to wake you. He said to take your time; he won't be back for a while so feel free to use the bathroom here before you go back to your own room.'

The whole scenario was surreal. Elfie wondered if she was dreaming. 'Sasha, what's going on? Why didn't he wake me before he left?'

Sasha looked at her in surprise. 'Well he was up early — he always rises at six. He usually leaves the morning stuff to me.'

Elfie felt faint. 'What morning stuff?'

165

'The breakfast and tidying up . . . you know . . . the 'morning after' . . . ' She stared at Elfie as her lips curled slowly. 'Oh, dear. You thought you were the only one?' Elfie said nothing. Sasha frowned in sympathy. 'I'm so sorry; I assumed you knew what he was like.'

'He does this often?' Elfie managed to say.

The PA shrugged. 'It varies. He travels a lot so I suppose it's difficult for him to form a real relationship. But men have needs, don't they?'

Elfie leaned against the wall, suddenly feeling in need of its support. Her heart thudded in her ears. Was Sasha deliberately misleading her, purposefully being cruel to get her out of the way?

But then Sasha said something that showed Elfie that the PA had definitely spoken to Gabriel that morning. 'He said he had left something on your pillow for you. That it was yours to keep in memory of him, if you wanted it.' She looked at the bed curiously. 'What was it?'

Elfie still held the Buckle. She opened her hand and looked at it. She thought about the ridiculous myth that surrounded it. Suddenly she wanted to cry. He'd slept with her, and now he wanted her out. He hadn't even had the grace to say goodbye.

'Are you okay?' Sasha came over, concerned. 'You look awfully white.' She looked at the Buckle and gave Elfie a small smile. 'He must have really liked you. He only ever gave his other women flowers.'

Elfie bit her lip hard. She would not cry in front of this woman. She turned and put the Buckle on the dressing table. 'You can tell him to keep this. He can put it in his museum. I don't want it.'

Sasha shrugged. 'Okay. At least everyone can come and see it then.' She picked the artefact up. 'He so wants the museum to be a success and I do hope it is. Perhaps then he can put the ghost of Juliet to rest.

'It doesn't sound like he's had much trouble doing that,' Elfie said softly.

Sasha gave a harsh laugh. 'She's all he thinks about. I'm not surprised you feel angry at him. I would too. To know you're just a temporary replacement for a dead woman . . . ' She frowned. 'You'd think after all the women he's been with he would have got over her by now.'

Elfie felt sick. She walked over and picked up her coat and bag. 'Say goodbye to him for me.'

Sasha looked at her in alarm. 'Where are you going? Aren't you going to stay until he gets back?'

'I think it would be best if I leave now, don't you?' Elfie whispered. She walked past Sasha, out of the door and let herself in her own room.

Inside, she began to stuff her clothes into her case. Hot tears poured down her face, but she hardly noticed them. How could she have been so stupid? She had only known him for two days, for crying out loud, what was she expecting? Lifelong commitment? A proposal?

She laughed out loud, but it came out as a sob. She pressed shaking fingers to her mouth, then hurriedly continued packing. She was idiotic and naive; she deserved everything she got. Perhaps now she had learned why she should never fall in love.

Only it was too late, of course. The Buckle had worked its magic, and she had fallen for him, opening her heart to the dagger of betrayal that now twisted deep inside. Suddenly she knew how her mother must have felt — and her parents' relationship had been years old, not days. How much worse had it been for her mother?

Elfie picked up the green dress. It personified everything that had happened that weekend. Her terrible weakness; his ultimate treachery.

Or was it — had he promised anything that he hadn't delivered? He had never said he was interested in a relationship, never said he loved her. Why would he? He had only known her two days. She had only herself to blame.

But deep down she knew that wasn't the whole story. He had led her to believe she was special; that she held a priceless spot in his heart, in spite of their brief relationship. He had made her feel extraordinary, unique; he had seemed to see through her to the deepest parts of her soul that she had thought hidden. He had understood her, had found the seed of her vulnerability and nourished it, brought it to bloom. And now he was leaving it to wither and die.

Elfie left the dress and wrap hanging over a chair. She grabbed her old jacket and suitcase and left the room without a backward glance.

10

Two weeks later it was Christmas Eve and Elfie was in Canterbury, visiting its magnificent cathedral. Outside, for the first time that she could remember in years, it was snowing. It wasn't quite the thick, beautiful snow of Prague, it was more like wet slush, but it still had children squealing and running out into the streets to play.

Inside the Cathedral, however, it was quiet and dry. It was after eleven o'clock, but not quite time for midnight mass, so although there were a few people about, it was hardly bustling.

She was standing at the site of Thomas Becket's murder, having walked around the church down the south aisle, round the Trinity Chapel and back up the north. Now she stopped to light a votive candle. *Who am I lighting it for?* she wondered as she touched the wick to its neighbour. Her father, her mother, hoping that she had at last found peace, but mostly she was lighting it for herself.

It had been a rough two weeks. After Sasha found her that morning in the hotel room, Elfie had left immediately, catching a taxi to the airport. Although the weather had been bad the previous night it had stopped snowing and she had been able to get a last-minute flight to England, to her relief. She didn't want to stay one more night in the city that had betrayed her.

Back home, she rang work on Monday and told David Parsons that she was unwell and wouldn't be in for the rest of the week. She hadn't had any sick leave for the past several years so he didn't complain. He did ask how the trip to Prague went. She told him it was successful and that they had found the Buckle. He seemed to catch her tone of voice and didn't ask anything else.

After that, she started doing some ringing around. Eventually she found what she wanted; a small country cottage in Kent that had just had a cancellation for the pre-Christmas weeks.

Once again Elfie packed her bags and left. She spent her time wandering around historical sites in the south east; Dover Castle, Hever, Leeds, Reculver. Every day she immersed herself in the history that she loved, trying to let it wash over her and wipe away her unhappiness.

But it didn't work.

And so here she was on Christmas Eve, in Canterbury Cathedral, miserable and at the end of her tether. Elfie wasn't religious, but she did hope that somehow she might be able to soak up some of the peaceful atmosphere of the building.

Leaving Becket's area behind, the site of the ancient murder sending a shiver up her spine, she went into the lighter nave and sat in one of the seats. It was colder there and she huddled in her coat, her hands in her pockets. Around her, people came and went, tourists admiring the beauty of the old building, choirboys and church men getting ready for midnight mass.

Elfie felt tired. She hadn't slept well since returning from Prague and she was exhausted. She had hardly eaten, and she knew she had dark shadows under her eyes.

She leaned forward and put her face in her hands. She just wanted to forget. Forget and move on. Put it all behind her. Please, she begged whoever was listening. Please help me get over him. I can't carry on like this.

Still leaning forward, she wiped her face, opening her eyes. She felt more than saw the person standing just a few feet away from her. She turned and saw black shoes, dark jeans, a long black coat . . . She looked up.

For a moment she just stared, thinking she was dreaming, that she had somehow conjured him up. Then she realised how different he looked and knew he was real. He was unshaven, with two weeks' growth of beard; his hair was damp with snow. He looked like he had lost weight. His hands were shoved deep in his pockets. He was staring at her as if he, too, couldn't believe she was there.

She stood hurriedly, almost knocking the chair over in the process, and backed away a couple of feet. Her heart was pounding.

'Please,' said Gabriel, stepping forward. 'Please don't go. It's taken me so long to find you.' He looked genuinely worried that she would flee like a frightened deer in the forest.

'What are you doing here?' Her voice was just a whisper.

'I came to find you.'

'How did you know where I was?'

He gave a laugh, but there was no humour in it. 'Well I knew you'd be somewhere historical. But it's pure luck I picked here, tonight.'

She stared at him. 'You're here by chance?'

'Well, not quite. I found out you were staying around here. I've been going round all the castles, all the sites I could think of in the area. David knew you were going to the south-east. He told me Canterbury was one of your favourite places. I thought you'd show up here eventually.'

Her head was spinning. 'I don't understand why you're here.'

He took a step closer, then stopped as she backed away. 'I needed to see you, to explain.'

'Explain what?' she said hotly. 'I think it's all perfectly clear.'

'No,' he said, forcefully this time. 'You don't know the whole story.'

'I know that when I woke up in that hotel room, you had left without even saying goodbye.'

He closed his eyes briefly. 'That part, at least, is true. And I've cursed myself every day for it.'

'I don't want to hear this,' she said, turning away. She began to walk down the aisle of chairs. He moved after her, however, grabbing her arm and turning her round. 'Get off me!' She snatched her arm away, eyes blazing.

He glared at her. 'I'm not letting you go until you hear what I have to say.'

'You have no right to tell me what to do!' She was shaking now.

'I know.' He held his hands up. His eyes were full of anguish. 'But please, Elfie, hear me out and if you still want to go, I won't stop you.'

She didn't want to listen, didn't want to hear him say he was sorry. Why had he come? Why couldn't he leave her alone?

But she knew that, short of making a terrible scene in the middle of the Cathedral, which was slowly beginning to fill with people, she couldn't walk away. She sank into one of the chairs, suddenly tired, took off her glasses and put them in her pocket and rubbed her eyes. Clearly relieved that she had decided to stay, he sat beside her, leaving one free chair between them.

'Well? What have you got to say that's so important?'

Suddenly he seemed lost for words.

'I've gone through this so many times in my head,' he admitted. 'But now I don't know where to start.'

'How about you tell me what was so important that you had to leave me without saying goodbye?'

He nodded. 'Okay. At around six in the morning, I got a text on my phone. I'd left it beside the bed and it woke me. It said that there had been an accident, and Tesar's wife had been badly hurt.'

'Tesar? Your driver?'

'Yes. He'd left his home to go to work — he normally picks me up at six thirty to take me to the office.'

'It was Sunday.'

He shrugged. 'I usually catch up on things in the office on Sundays as it's quieter. I wasn't actually going to go in that morning, but I'd forgotten to tell him. His wife had got up earlier as she was going on a long trip to visit her sister, who'd just gone into labour. She took their car and skidded in the snow, right into an oncoming lorry.'

Elfie was shivering, although she didn't know if it was cold or the shock of what he was saying. 'Is she okay?'

'Broken a gazillion bones; all sorts of internal bleeding. She'll be in hospital for a while but at least she's alive.'

Elfie frowned, thinking of the way his driver had sat patiently in the shop passing comment on her outfits. 'Poor Tesar,' she whispered.

'I know. As soon as I read the text, I knew I had to be the one to tell him. They didn't want to phone him in case he was driving at the time. I thought I was coming back — I didn't wake you because you were sound asleep and you looked so lovely, lying there. I left the Buckle on the pillow, just in case you woke up while I was out.'

Elfie bit her lip, not looking at him, at his lovely, warm brown eyes. Don't cry, she urged herself.

'I went downstairs and he'd just pulled up outside. I went straight out and told him. He was distraught, of course; he wanted to drive to the

179

hospital there and then. I knew he couldn't; that he'd just have an accident himself in that state. I had to wrestle the keys out of his hand. His brother was coming to pick him up, but he lived an hour away and Tesar couldn't wait. In the end, I told him I'd drive him.'

He ran a hand through his damp hair. 'I nipped back into the hotel. I asked the concierge to order a dozen red roses and I quickly wrote a note to you, explaining everything, before I left.'

Elfie stared at him. 'But . . . '

'I know.' His eyes were full of anger. 'I found out that, after I'd left, Sasha came downstairs. She found the flowers and the note and told the concierge that I'd rung her and asked her to deliver them. But she didn't, of course. She read the note — that's how she knew I'd left you the Buckle — then threw the note and the flowers away.'

She studied him, shocked. 'She lied to me?'

'Total fabrication. She admitted it all,

said she'd done it for me, that she was waiting for me . . . I've no idea why, I've never given her any indication that I'd be interested in her. I sacked her anyway, of course. I couldn't believe what she'd done, that she'd ruined the only good thing that had happened in my life for years.' A hint of a smile hovered on his lips.

Elfie couldn't return it. Her throat had tightened so much that she had trouble swallowing. 'She said that she always sorted out the morning stuff — with all your women.'

For the first time real amusement lit his face. 'All my women? Elfie, sweetheart, you are the first woman I've been with since Juliet died.' Tentatively, afraid she'd pull away, he took her hand. 'I know we'd only known each other two days. It happened too quickly. We should have spent longer getting to know each other. Perhaps it was the romance of the city, perhaps it was the Buckle.' He smiled wryly. 'All I know is that I fell in love with you the moment

I saw you in the lecture theatre.'

A tear ran down her cheek and she pulled her hand away. 'Don't, Gabriel, I can't get involved with a man who is still in love with another woman, even if she is dead.'

He studied her. Then he looked down at his hands. 'There is something I haven't told you,' he said softly. 'Before Juliet told me she was having an affair, I was planning to leave her. You've got to understand, we met when we were quite young. She was beautiful but in an unobtainable way. I was just beginning to make the business successful, I was going to a lot of official parties and she came from a wealthy family and had lots of connections. She wanted a man she could show off and, at the time, I fitted the bill. We suited each other, then, but . . . '

He ran both hands through his hair, then leaned forward, elbows on knees. 'As the years went by, though, I began to realise that we were very different people. She was . . . shallow.' He shook his head. 'No, that's unfair. She was just interested in different things to me. She loved fashion and celebrities and interior design, stuff that I didn't give a damn about. History had always been important to me, and she hated anything to do with archaeology and artefacts.' He looked across at Elfie and gave a wry smile. 'Ironic really, considering I'm opening a museum in her name.'

Elfie said nothing. Her head was whirling.

'Anyway,' he continued, 'the six months before she found out she was ill, I'd really begun to have second thoughts. I was unhappy — we weren't connecting at all and she wasn't interested in anything important to me.'

He studied his hands again and cleared his throat. 'After I introduced her to Doležal, I began to suspect that she was seeing him, but the terrible thing was, I didn't really care. I planned to confront her about her affair then I could tell her we were over; I'd have an excuse, see? I'm a weak man, Elfie. Not the stuff of Shakespearean heroes.'

'What happened?' she whispered.

'The day I'd planned to tell her, she came home a broken woman. She'd found out she had cancer — I didn't even know she'd gone for tests, that's how little we were communicating — and she'd gone to Doležal and told him but he'd thrown her out. She told me everything; that she was pregnant but that she hadn't told him, that she was going to have to abort the baby, and that she was very sick and probably wouldn't recover. She begged me to let her stay until the end, because she didn't want to be alone.'

'And you said yes.'

He nodded. 'I couldn't just finish it there. She was my wife, after all.'

Her heart went out to him. 'I understand.'

He took a deep breath and let it out slowly. 'So I hired nurses to look after her and made sure that she didn't want for anything, and I was there at the end.' He sighed. 'But our marriage had ended long before she died. Both the men in her life had let her down. I created the museum for her because I felt she deserved something.'

He looked across at her. Unshed tears brightened his brown eyes to polished mahogany. 'I'm sorry I didn't tell you before. But I didn't want you to think I was a heel. I wanted you to like me.'

She gave a small smile. 'You looked after your wife when other men might have turned their backs, Gabriel. How could I think badly of you?' Hope momentarily lit his face, but she shook her head sadly. 'I'm glad you finally explained everything to me, but it still doesn't change anything.'

'I don't understand . . . '

'Even if it wasn't your fault, what happened in Prague broke my heart. I've promised myself since my father died that I would never allow that to happen to me. And that was before I realised how much emotional pain a person could feel. I couldn't go through it again, Gabriel, I just won't.'

'I'm not asking you to. I'm asking you to give us a chance. You have to admit we had something magical, albeit brief. Don't you wonder what it would be like to let it develop?'

She shook her head again. 'You can't promise me a happy ending. We don't know how it would work out.'

He frowned with frustration. 'But that's life, sweetheart. There are no promises about anything. Love is all about taking a chance.'

Elfie stood. Her bottom lip was trembling. 'I'm sorry, Gabriel. I can't.'

He rose slowly, looking distraught. 'This can't be it. Not now I've found you again. I haven't stopped looking for you since I came back to the hotel and realised you'd gone.

Tears broke over the rim of her eyes and rolled down her face. 'Please don't, this is hard enough . . . '

He stepped forward and put his arms around her. 'I can't believe this is it.' His voice cracked with emotion.

In the background, the choir suddenly started singing. It was about eleven forty-five, she realised, and they were welcoming people in for midnight mass. Their voices rang out, clear and pure, through the nave.

He pulled back and looked down at her. His eyes had dark smudges under them. He had probably slept as little as she had since they parted, she thought. His face was wet from his own tears as he bent his head and gave her a long kiss on her forehead, then her cheeks. He looked at her again, deep into her eyes. Finally, he kissed her lips.

His mouth was soft, his lips cool and oh, so tender, his beard a sensual, unfamiliar brush. Against her will, her head tipped back and she leaned into him, welcoming this final kiss.

To her right, she caught a movement out of the corner of her eye. She pulled back and looked over, seeing a little old lady standing watching them. Elfie wiped her tears hurriedly, suddenly conscious that several people in the nave were casting glances at them.

The old lady smiled. 'The angels are singing for you both, my dear. What a wonderful place to be kissing the man you love.' She carried on walking down the aisle, looking up at the architecture.

Elfie looked back at Gabriel. His arms were still tight around her. She swallowed. 'I . . . '

'Don't say anything.' He kissed her again, a long, lingering kiss that began to make her heart beat a little faster.

When he lifted his head, she blinked at him. 'Gabriel, I . . . ' He kissed her again. This time she pulled back, giving a short laugh of exasperation. 'Are you going to keep kissing me until I give in?'

'If that's what it takes.' He cradled her head, pressed her against him and kissed her for a fourth time, lingeringly

Elfie pushed back, scarlet-faced. Gabriel smiled at the couple who were giving them the thumbs up as they passed. He looked back at her, his brown eyes now much warmer. He held her face, his thumbs brushing her cheeks. 'Don't push me away,' he whispered.

'You still think you can get something if you want it enough,' she said. 'I can't be bought, Gabriel. I can't be kept by sheer willpower.'

'I know. But I'm willing to take that risk. If it doesn't work out, it won't be for the want of trying, believe me. But it might work out, it just might. I won't rush you, but shouldn't we give it a chance? What's it all about, if it's not about trying to find real love?'

He was so gorgeous, she thought, even with two weeks' worth of beard. Was it really possible that she could spend the rest of her life with him?

Everything Sasha had told her had been a lie. He hadn't let her down at all; he had left her in bed that morning to help out a friend and it was the PA who had ruined everything. Elfie knew she wasn't just one of many women — she was the only one he'd been with for a year and a half. She didn't doubt that everything he'd said was the truth.

Suddenly he fumbled in his coat

pocket. 'I have something here that may convince you.' He pulled out a glowing gold item and placed it in her hand. It was the Buckle. 'Charlemagne wants you to give us a chance,' he whispered. 'And Libuse. They couldn't be together, but they are hoping that we can end the dream for them the way it should end.'

She clutched the artefact. True love, she thought. Perhaps it was possible, after all. She looked up at him. She couldn't say anything; she hoped that her eyes said it all.

Gabriel — the archangel of her dreams — wrapped her in his arms and kissed her exultantly as the bells began to ring for midnight mass.

THE END

We do hope that you have enjoyed reading this large print book.

Did you know that all of our titles are available for purchase?

We publish a wide range of high quality large print books including:
Romances, Mysteries, Classics
General Fiction
Non Fiction and Westerns

Special interest titles available in large print are:
The Little Oxford Dictionary
Music Book, Song Book
Hymn Book, Service Book

Also available from us courtesy of Oxford University Press:
Young Readers' Dictionary
(large print edition)
Young Readers' Thesaurus
(large print edition)

For further information or a free brochure, please contact us at:
Ulverscroft Large Print Books Ltd.,
The Green, Bradgate Road, Anstey,
Leicester, LE7 7FU, England.
Tel: (00 44) **0116 236 4325**
Fax: (00 44) **0116 234 0205**

EARL GRESHAM'S BRIDE

Angela Drake

When heiress Kate Roscoe compromises herself through an innocent mistake, widower, Earl Gresham steps in with an offer of marriage to save her reputation. She is soon deeply in love with him, but is beset by the problems of overseeing his grand household. The housekeeper is dishonest and the nanny of the earl's two children is heartless and lazy. But a far greater threat comes from his former mistress who will go to any lengths to destroy Kate's marriage.

FINDING ANNABEL

Paula Williams

Annabel had disappeared after going to meet the woman who, she'd just discovered, was her natural mother . . . However, when her sister Jo travels to Somerset to try and find her, she must follow a trail of lies and deceit. The events of the past and the present have become dangerously entangled. And she discovers, to her cost, that for some people in the tiny village of Neston Parva, old loyalties remain fierce and strangers are not welcome . . .

IT WAS ALWAYS YOU

Miranda Barnes

Anna Fenwick is very fond of Matthew, a hard-working young man from her Northumberland village. She has known him all her life, although, sadly, it seems that he is not interested in her. Then Anna embarks on a whirlwind romance with Don, a visiting Canadian and goes to Calgary with him. Life is wonderful for a time. However, her heart is still in Northumberland — but when she returns to seek Matthew, will she eventually find him?